GONE, GONE, GONE

ALSO BY HANNAH MOSKOWITZ

Invincible Summer

Break

GONE, GONE, GONE

HANNAH MOSKOWITZ

SIMON PULSE

NEW YORK   LONDON   TORONTO   SYDNEY   NEW DELHI

SIMON PULSE

An imprint of Simon & Schuster Children's Publishing Division
1230 Avenue of the Americas, New York, NY 10020
First Simon Pulse edition April 2012
Copyright © 2012 by Hannah Moskowitz
All rights reserved, including the right of reproduction
in whole or in part in any form.
SIMON PULSE and colophon are registered trademarks
of Simon & Schuster, Inc.
For information about special discounts for bulk purchases,
please contact Simon & Schuster Special Sales at 1-866-506-1949
or business@simonandschuster.com.
The Simon & Schuster Speakers Bureau can bring authors
to your live event. For more information or to book an event contact the
Simon & Schuster Speakers Bureau at 1-866-248-3049
or visit our website at www.simonspeakers.com.
Designed by Mike Rosamilia
The text of this book was set in ITC New Baskerville.
Manufactured in the United States of America
2 4 6 8 10 9 7 5 3 1
Library of Congress Control Number 2011935726
ISBN 978-1-4424-5312-8 (hc)
ISBN 978-1-4424-0753-4 (pbk)
ISBN 978-1-4424-0754-1 (eBook)

To the survivors

GONE, GONE, GONE

CRAIG

I WAKE UP TO A QUIET WORLD.

There's this stillness so strong that I can feel it in the hairs on the backs of my arms, and I can right away tell that this quiet is the sound of a million things and fourteen bodies not here and one boy breathing alone.

I open my eyes.

I can't believe I slept.

I sit up and swing my feet to the floor. I'm wearing my shoes, and I'm staring at them like I don't recognize them, but they're the shoes I wear all the time, these black canvas high-tops from Target. My mom bought them for me. I have that kind of mom.

I can feel how cold the tile is. I can feel it through my shoes.

I make kissing noises with my mouth. Nothing answers. My brain is telling me, my brain has been telling me for every single second since I woke up, exactly what is different, but I am not going to think it, I won't think it, because they're all just hiding or upstairs. They're not gone. The only thing in the whole world I am looking at is my shoes, because everything else is exactly how it's supposed to be, because they're not gone.

But this, this is wrong. That I'm wearing shoes. That I slept in my shoes. I think it says something about you when you don't even untie your shoes to try to go to bed. I think it's a dead giveaway that you are a zombie. If there is a line between zombie and garden-variety insomniac, that line is a shoelace.

I got the word "zombie" from my brother Todd. He calls me "zombie," sometimes, when he comes home from work at three in the morning—Todd is so old, old enough to work night shifts and drink coffee without sugar—and comes down to the basement to check on me. He walks slowly, one hand on the banister, a page of the newspaper crinkling in his hand. He won't flick on the light, just in case I'm asleep, and there I am, I'm on the couch, a cat on each of my shoulders and a man with a small penis on the TV telling me how he became a man with a big penis, and I can too. "Zombie," Todd will say softly, a hand on top of my head. "Go to sleep."

Todd has this way of being affectionate that I see but usually don't feel.

I say, "Someday I might need this."

"The penis product?"

"Yes." Maybe not. I think my glory days are behind me. I am fifteen years old, and all I have is the vague hope that, someday, someone somewhere will once again care about my penis and whether it is big or small.

The cats don't care. Neither do my four dogs, my three rabbits, my guinea pig, or even the bird I call Flamingo because he stands on one leg when he drinks, even though that isn't his real name, which is Fernando.

They don't care. And even if they did, they're not here. I can't avoid that fact any longer.

I am the vaguest of vague hopes of a deflated heart.

I look around the basement, where I sleep now. My alarm goes off, even though I'm already up. The animals should be scuffling around now that they hear I'm awake, mewing, rubbing against my legs, and whining for food. This morning, the alarm is set for five thirty for school, and my bedroom is a silent, frozen meat locker because the animals are gone.

Here's what happened, my parents explain, weary over cups of coffee, cops come and gone, all while I was asleep.

What happened is that I slept.

I slept through a break-in and a break-out, but I couldn't sleep through the quiet afterward. This has to be a metaphor for something, but I can't think, it's too quiet.

Broken window, jimmied locks. They took the upstairs TV and parts of the stereo. They left all the doors open. The house is as cold as October. The animals are gone.

It was a freak accident. Freak things happen. I should be used to that by now. Freaks freaks freaks.

Todd was the one to come home and discover the damage. My parents slept through it too. This house is too big.

I say, "But the break-in must have been hours ago."

My mother nods a bit.

I say, "Why didn't I wake up as soon as the animals escaped?"

My mom doesn't understand what I'm talking about, but this isn't making sense to me. None of it is. Break-ins aren't supposed to happen to us. We live in a nice neighborhood in a nice suburb. They're supposed to happen to other people. I am supposed to be so tied to the happiness and the comfort of those animals that I can't sleep until every single one is fed, cleaned, hugged. Maybe if I find enough flaws in this, I can make it so it never happened.

This couldn't have happened.

At night, Sandwich and Carolina and Zebra sleep down at my feet. Flamingo goes quiet as soon as I put a sheet over his cage. Peggy snuggles in between my arm and my body. Caramel won't settle down until he's tried and failed, at least four or five times, to fall asleep right on my face. Shamrock always sleeps on the couch downstairs, no matter how many times I try to settle him on the bed with me, and Marigold has a spot under the window that she really likes, but sometimes she sleeps in her kennel instead, and I can never find Michelangelo in the morning and it always scares me, but he always turns up in my laundry basket or in the box with my tapes or under the bed, or sometimes he sneaks upstairs and sleeps with Todd, and the five others sleep all on top of each other in the corner on top of the extra comforter, but I checked all of those places this morning—every single one—and they're all gone, gone, gone.

Mom always tried to open windows because of the smell, but I'd stop her because I was afraid they would escape. Every day I breathe in feathers and dander and urine so they will not escape.

My mother sometimes curls her hand into a loose fist and presses her knuckles against my cheek. When she does, I smell her lotion, always lemongrass. Todd will do something similar, but it feels different, more urgent, when he does.

The animals. They were with me when I fell asleep last night. I didn't notice I was sleeping in my shoes, and I didn't notice when they left.

This is why I need more sleep. This is how things slip through my fingers.

My head is spinning with fourteen names I didn't protect.

"We'll find them, Craig," Mom says, with a hand on the back of my head. "They were probably just scared from the noise. They'll come back."

"They should have stayed in the basement," I whisper. "Why did they run away?"

Why were a few open doors enough incentive for them to leave?

I shouldn't have fallen asleep. I suck.

"We'll put up posters, Craig, okay?" Mom says. Like she doesn't have enough to worry about and people to call— insurance companies, someone to fix the window, and her mother to assure her that being this close to D.C. really doesn't mean we're going to die. It's been thirteen months, almost, since the terrorist attacks, and we're still convinced that any mishap means someone will steer a plane into one of our buildings.

We don't say that out loud.

Usually this time in the morning, I take all the different kinds of food and I fill all the bowls. They come running, tripping over themselves, rubbing against me, nipping my face and my hands like I am the food, like I just poured myself into a bowl and offered myself to them. Then I clean the litter boxes and the cages and take the dogs out for a walk.

I can do this all really, really quickly, after a year of practice.

Mom helps, usually, and sometimes I hear her counting under her breath, or staring at one of the animals, trying to figure out if one is new—sometimes yes, sometimes no.

The deal Mom and I have is no new animals. The deal is I don't have to give them away, I don't have to see a therapist, but I can't have any more animals. I don't want a therapist because therapists are stupid, and I am not crazy.

And the truth is it's not my fault. The animals find me. A kitten behind a Dumpster, a rabbit the girl at school can't keep. A dog too old for anyone to want. I just hope they find me again now that they're gone.

Part of the deal was also that Mom got to name a few of the newer ones, which is how I ended up with a few with really girly names.

But I love them. I tell them all the time. I'll pick Hail up and cuddle him to my face in that way that makes his ears get all twitchy. I'll make loose fists and hold them up to Marigold and Jupiter's cheeks. They'll lick my knuckles. "I love you," I tell them. It's always been really easy for me to say. I've never been one of those people who can't say it.

It's October 4th. Just starting to get cold, but it gets cold fast around here.

God, I hope they're okay.

I'm up way too early now that I don't have to feed the animals, but I don't know what else to do but get dressed and get ready for school. It takes like two minutes, and now what?

A year ago, back when it was still 2001 . . .
Back when we still clung . . .
Back when I slept upstairs . . .
There was a boy.
A very, very, very important boy.
Now . . .
There's Lio.
Lio. I knew how it was spelled before I ever heard it out loud. It sounds normal, like Leo, but it looks so special. I love that.

I started talking to Lio back in June. I'm this thing for my school called an ambassador, which basically means I get good grades and I don't smoke, so they give out my email and a little bit about me to incoming students so I can gush about how cool this place is or something like that.

He sent me a message. He said he's about to move here, he's going to be at my school, we're the same age, and this is so creepy stalker, but you like Jefferson Airplane and I like Jefferson Airplane too, so cool, do you think we could IM sometime?

So he did and we are and I do and we did.

Lio is, to sum him up quickly, a koala. I realized that pretty early on.

He gets good grades, but he smokes, so he could never be an ambassador. There are a few reasons it's really, really stupid for Lio to smoke, but that doesn't seem to stop him. I don't know him well enough to admit that it scares me to death. And really, it seems like everything scares me to death now, so I've learned to shut up about it.

He's not a *boy* to me, not yet, because *boy* implies some kind of intimacy, but Lio is a boy in the natural sense of the word, at least I assume so, since I've never seen him with his clothes off and barely with his coat off, to be honest. Though I can imagine. And sometimes I do. Oh, God.

He wears a lot of hats. That's how we met for real, once his family moved here. I thought he'd come looking for me as soon as school started, but I couldn't find him anywhere, which was immediately a shame, because I was beginning to get sick of eating my lunch alone every day.

Then Ms. Hoole made both of us take our hats off in honors precalculus last month, on the third day of school.

"Lio, Craig," she said. "Your hats, present them here." And of course I didn't give a shit about my hat, because I had found Lio.

Lio didn't say anything, but his eyes said, *bitch,* and when he took his hat off I could see his hair was a chopped-up mess of four different colors, all of them muted and faded and fraying. Lio has a head like an old couch.

After class, he didn't go up to collect his hat, so I got both and brought his to him. He was rushing down the hallway, unlit cigarette between his fingers.

I said, "Lio?"

He looked at me and nodded.

I smiled a bit. "You weren't listening? I'm Craig."

He bit his bottom lip like he was trying not to laugh, but not in a bad way. In a really, really warm way, and I could tell because his eyes were locked onto mine.

There was a whole mess of people and he was still walking, but he kept looking at me.

"I like your hair," I told him, because it was difficult not to make some sort of comment.

Lio leaned against the wall and studied me. And even though I know now that Lio's really uncomfortable without a hat on, and he was really mad at Ms. Hoole for taking it and really mad at himself for being too afraid of talking to go up and ask for it back, he didn't pull the hat back on right away. He kept it crumpled up in his hand and he watched me instead.

And he covered his mouth a little and he smiled.

So here are some facts about Lio:

He has either five or six older sisters, I can't remember,

and one younger sister, and they are all very nice and love him a lot and call him nearly every day, except for his little sister, Michelle, and the youngest of the older sisters, Jasper, who are in middle school and high school, respectively, and therefore live with him and therefore only call him when he's in trouble or they want to borrow his clothes. I've only met Jasper. She is a senior, and much prettier than Lio. They all have cell phones, every single one of them, because they are from New York, and Lio says everyone has them there, and I don't know if that's true, but I'm really jealous.

He likes Colin Farrell, so when that movie *Phone Booth* comes out next month, we're going to go see it together. I don't know if this is a date or what, but I've already decided that I'm going to pay, and if he tries to protest I'm going to give him this smile and be like "No, no, let me."

He used to be a cancer kid—bald, skinny, mouth sores, leukemia. That was when he was five until he was seven, I think. He got to go to Alaska to see polar bears because of the Make-A-Wish Foundation. He said one time that the thing about cancer kids is no one knows what to do with them if they don't die. He's fine now, but he shouldn't be smoking cigarettes. He had a twin brother who died.

Today I come up to Lio's locker and he nods to me. The principal gave us American flags to put up on our lockers on September 11th, for the anniversary. Most of us put them up, but we also took them down again afterward, because they were cheap and flimsy and because it's been a year and patriotism is lame again. Lio still has his on his locker, but three weeks later it's started to fray. My father gave his school flags too. He's an elementary school principal. My mother is a social worker. My family is a little adorable.

Lio's flag flaps while he roots through his locker. He takes out a very small cage and hands it to me. I'm excited for a minute, thinking he's found one of the animals, maybe Peggy, the guinea pig. Even though there's no way she could fit in there, I'm still hoping, because maybe maybe maybe. But it's a small white mouse. Really, really pretty.

But it makes my head immediately list everyone that I've lost.

Four dogs: Jupiter, Casablanca, Kremlin, Marigold.

Five cats: Beaumont, Zebra, Shamrock, Sandwich, Caramel.

One bird: Fernando.

Three rabbits: Carolina, Hail, Michelangelo.

A guinea pig: Peggy.

"Made me think of you," he says, softly.

Because Lio says so few words, every single one has deep, metaphorical, cosmic significance in my life. And my words are like pennies.

I talk to the mouse very quietly on my way back to my

locker. I think I'll name her Zippers. I'm not sure why. I'm never sure why I choose the names I do. Maybe I should let Mom handle all of them, although she'd probably name this one Princess or something.

I should ask Lio what he'd like her to be named. Or where he got her. He doesn't know about the deal I have with my mom, and I feel no need to tell him.

I set her cage on top of my books.

Lio's there a minute later. He bites his thumbnail and fusses with his hat. His hair's still a mess, but it has nothing to do with the cancer. He's just sort of a psycho with his hair.

"My therapist says I'm a little fucked up," he explained to me one time, when I barely knew him, and that explanation terrified and intrigued me all at the same time. He sniffled and rubbed his nose. "Yeah."

Once I told him therapy is bullshit and he seemed offended, so I don't tell him that anymore, even though I still believe it.

"My animals are gone," I tell him now.

He looks up.

"Someone broke into my house last night. They broke the windows and left all the doors open, and all my animals left. They just ran out the doors or something . . ."

He watches me. Sometimes he does this, looks at me when I'm in the middle of talking, and it's like he's interrupting without saying a word, because I can't think with

13

those eyes all blue on me. I can't think of anything else to say, and it makes me want to cry. Usually I can handle this, because I'm only talking about my brother or a class or my day. But right now it's a little more than I can stand.

I need Lio to say something.

But he doesn't. He reaches out and touches the tip of my finger with the tip of his finger.

Bing.

I swallow.

He says, "Did you look under the couch?"

Even stuff like that sounds profound from him, and I hate that all I can do is nod while I'm trying to get my voice back, because I always like to give Lio more of a response when he talks to me, since it's so hard to get words out of him.

"Yeah," I say eventually. "We looked under the couch."

"I'm sorry."

Lio's never seen my animals because he's never been to my house, but he's heard enough about them. Plus there are pictures of them all over my locker. I touch a Polaroid of Jemeena, this excellent hamster I had who died a few months ago. I couldn't bring myself to get any more hamsters after her.

I look at Lio.

I haven't been to Lio's place either. He says it's still full of boxes, because their apartment is so big that they don't even notice them taking up space. I think he's just used to his old tiny apartment in New York.

"I need to put up posters after school," I tell Lio. "Will you come help me?"

He nods.

"Thanks." The bell goes off and I close my locker door. "I hope they're still alive."

"It's not cold yet."

He probably wouldn't say that if he'd gone a whole night with wind pouring into his house. Getting out of the shower felt like a punishment. I say, "I know. They could probably have survived last night, I hope. What if maybe someone stole them off the street? I hope not." I breathe out.

He nods a little. "We'll find them."

We start walking to class, and this girl passing us waves to Lio, this tall blond girl with glasses and a pretty smile.

I say, "She'd be really hot if she were a boy."

Lio watches her go and nods slowly. I wish I knew what that meant. It would be something else to think about.

Todd is at my locker after second period. He substitute teaches here sometimes, so it's not that weird to see him, even though I didn't know he was working today. The substitute teaching thing isn't his real job. Really, he works nights at a suicide hotline, which pays even less than substitute teaching. He's taking classes to get his masters in environmental science. Then he's going to save us all before the world explodes.

He holds up a paper bag. "You forgot your lunch."

This is why people need sleep. "Thanks," I say. I bet Mom made him bring it to me. She's pretty intense about lunch. She still packs mine every day, because she wants me to get a lot of vitamins or whatever. I usually end up giving half of it to Lio and eating chips instead. I'm not going to tell Todd that.

"You doing okay?" he asks.

"What?"

He says, "Just checking in," and he gives me a hug with one arm and then leaves. I open my lunch bag like I think there's going to be some explanation of why he was so affectionate, I guess because I wish it were something better than *because he feels sorry for you and your lost animals.* But it's just an apple and a sandwich and a bag of walnuts. I rip off a bit of the apple for Zippers and stuff everything else into my locker before I head off to my next class.

Lio is against the wall, standing with some girls that he is half friends with. It's probably hard to be friends with a kid that quiet, but I wouldn't know, because it's been very easy for me to be whatever Lio and I are.

He smiles at me with the corner of his mouth when I walk up. I give him the smallest little kick above his shoe.

"Has Lio been entertaining you with his witty banter?" I ask.

The girls look uncomfortable, like they think maybe I'm being mean. Lio looks away from me, but his smile is a little bigger now. Heh. I couldn't even tell you what any of these girls looks like, or whether I'd like any of them if they were boys.

Silver Spring is a half city in the same way Lio is a half koala. Lately they've been developing it more and more— sticking in Whole Foods and rich hippie stuff like that, and they started redoing the metro station so it's easier to get downtown, which my parents say doesn't matter because there's no way I'm riding the metro alone until I stop tripping over my feet and talking to strangers. But I guess it's okay as long as I'm with Lio. I didn't ask.

We're at the Glenmont station now, me and Lio, to put up signs. MANY MISSING PETS. DOGS, CATS, SMALL ANIMALS. PLEASE CALL. REWARD.

FOUR DOGS

FIVE CATS

ONE BIRD

THREE RABBITS

A GUINEA PIG

I don't know what I'm going to do about a reward. The mouse Lio gave me makes tiny chirping noises in my backpack. I make sure she's safe in there, and she gets another bit of apple for being so good all day.

In the corner a man plays a harmonica, but he has an empty guitar case in front of him to collect money. He looks sort of like Lio—very small with big hands, a little grungy.

Lio isn't exactly grungy, but he's definitely more hardcore something than I am. At least, he's into ironic T-shirts—the one he's wearing now has a picture of a football with SOCCER over it—and jeans that sit too low on his hips. Usually black ones. I'm either preppier or lazier. I still wear the kind of clothes my mom said looked good on me when I was ten. Except I've grown nearly a foot since then, so I look older than fifteen, but I feel younger, and I think that's a big source of trouble for me.

It's five o'clock, and this is the last station we're covering today. Our hands are sore from stapling up posters, and we're still a little red because one of the guards at Shady Grove yelled at us and asked us if we had a permit or something. At every other station, we were left alone. It figures. I've never met a nice person at Shady Grove, ever.

We go up the escalator and into the outdoor area underneath the awning. "We could catch a bus," Lio says, though I don't know why, because I assume we're going to get on the metro and go back to Forest Glen, where I live, and he already said his dad would pick him up, no problem. I would be excited about the idea that he's coming home with me if it didn't mean that he was going to see my house without animals, so I made up some lie about how my parents don't let me invite friends in when they're not there so we'll just have to wait on the porch until his dad gets there, and I think maybe he knew I was lying and maybe he thinks I don't want him there. But it's just because of the animals. That's all it is.

It's just that I haven't invited anyone in for a really long time, I guess.

Anyway, there's no reason either of us should catch a bus.

Then he says, "We could get on a bus and go really far away."

I put my hand on his back. "Like New York?"

"Like outer space." He stiffens a little under my hand, so I take it away.

I try not to think about it, but I really don't know what I'm doing with Lio. I guess we're friends, sort of, except we don't really talk. We're the closest either one of us has to a friend, because I can't stand most people anymore and Lio left all the people who were used to him in New York, and it's pretty damn depressing until you consider that I really like being with Lio, and I hope he likes being with me. And we do spend a lot of time together. I don't know if Lio's into boys. It seems like a stupid question, because I don't know what difference the answer will make. The question isn't whether he's into boys. The question is if he's into me. I know lots of gay boys, after all—I'm in drama club—but here I am without a boyfriend.

It's starting to get dark. If the clocks had changed already, it would be Todd-coffee black out here by now. I guess we're lucky.

There are two guys, definitely older than us, slumming on the gate that separates the metro station from the church. Actually, they're not slumming. One of them is sitting on the gate and the other is swinging it back and forth, like he's rocking him to sleep. Except they're laughing.

A part of me loves Glenmont. I love the water tower here so much more than the one back at Forest Glen, which is short and fat and always looks like it's watching everything. Here, everything's dirty in a beautiful way. Grimy, I guess, is the word I'm looking for. Everything's covered and maybe protected by a layer of grime. I wish we went to school here instead of in Forest Glen, where all the houses and schools are tucked into little neighborhoods, like we have to hide. My school and my house are both in that one part of town, so it's like I can't ever get out of it.

"There's no way the animals would have gotten this far," I say. "They don't even know how to ride the metro. We should just go home and look there."

So we head back and get off the metro at Forest Glen and start walking toward my house. Todd's car is in the driveway. There goes my home-alone excuse.

"My brother can drive you home," I say.

He shakes his head. "Dad's coming at five fifteen."

"Oh."

"And it's, um, a little past five fifteen."

I guess that's good, because I don't think either he or Todd would really enjoy being stuck in a car together. Lio isn't known for responding well to normal social cues, never mind Todd's neurotic ones.

I guess I should invite Lio inside while we're waiting. That's not a big deal. It's just into the kitchen.

Lio says, "Craig."

I look up as he scurries under a bush and comes out with a little white kitten. Sandwich.

She's the newest of my animals. I was at the vet picking up antibiotics for Marigold, and she was there in a little box with four sisters, her eyes begging me, *hold me hold me hold me*, and I've never been able to resist that, ever, and now I take her from Lio and I have her. She's home. She didn't go far. She was just waiting for me.

She mews.

"Yours?" he asks.

I nod, because I'm not sure I can talk right now, or that I could say anything but Sandwich's name if I did. She's so dirty, and little bits of sticks cling to her. She looks up at me and mews again. I pet her cheek with my thumb, and then I give Lio a big smile.

21

He strokes her head for a minute, then says to me, very quietly, "Happy?"

I nod.

He leans in and kisses me.

It's soft and small. It's 5:20 p.m.

My parents decide we need to have BLTs with our pork chops in honor of Sandwich's return. It's weird, because we usually eat in front of the TV, but now we're all sitting at the table together, and it's so quiet without the news in the background or the animals underfoot.

Sandwich paws at my shoelace.

My father has this way of chewing that makes it look like a job. It's like he's considering every muscle in his jaw every time he uses it, like he's constantly reevaluating to make sure he's working at the right pace and pressure. When he was sixteen—only a year older than me, but when I imagine it he always looks twenty-five—he was a big-shot football player who got sidelined with a major head injury and had to do rehab and staples in his head and all of it. He and Lio should start a club of people who shouldn't be alive, and Mom and I can start a club of people who shouldn't be jealous but are, a little, because we will never really understand. My ex-boyfriend could be in that second club too. Or maybe he's my boyfriend. This isn't the kind of thing I want to think about.

Anyway, Dad says he recovered all the way, and Mom didn't meet him until years afterward, so we have to take his word for it, but whenever he does something weird like chew like a trash compactor or leave his keys in the refrigerator, I always picture these football-shaped neurons on his head struggling to connect to each other.

I can't believe Lio kissed me. Well, I can, but I think it's weird that he asked me "Happy?" first. If I had said no, would he have kissed me? Was it a reward for being happy, the same way I reward him when he talks? Was he thanking me for being happy?

It's been ten months since my last kiss. I don't know how long it's been since I've really been happy, but ten months is a good guess.

Todd rubs the skin between his eyes. I think his head is still bothering him.

Mom didn't have any luck finding the animals, but we're going to go back out tonight after dinner and keep looking. Mom says if Sandwich was out there, safe, the others must be too.

Dad says, "It's probably for the best."

I frown.

He says, "This isn't a barn, Craig. Maybe now you'll get out of the house, hmm? Start going out with your friends again."

"I don't have any friends."

"Are there any nice boys at school?" he says, in that way, and I guess I should be thankful that he says this no differently from how he asks Todd about girls at work, but I'm not, I just want him to pretend I'm a eunuch or something, especially since I pretty much am at this point, anyway.

Mom gives him a stern look. "We'll find them." She looks at me. "You know, your friend could have stayed for dinner." Now she's totally giving me a chance to tell her that Lio's more than a friend, and I have no idea what to say. The fact that my parents are entirely okay with my homosexuality makes talking about it kind of difficult, because when you're gay and single the only thing you have going for you is imagined shock value. The reality is that it's pretty boring to be like, *hey, parents, I'm gay, and there's absolutely no reason for you to give a shit right now.*

So I just say, "That's okay," and concentrate on cutting my pork chop.

And to be honest, calling Lio my friend seems wrong, probably because I don't remember, really, how to have friends. That sounds so pathetic, because I used to have friends, but then I had a boyfriend and sort of ignored everybody, and then after the boyfriend exploded I stopped being fun and started blowing people off when they asked me to hang out. It's not like everyone hates me, and I have people to talk to in classes but not once we're out in the halls, those sorts of friends. And I spend a lot of evenings here with the animals, and they were enough, in a way my parents could never appreciate and could barely tolerate.

Now what? Now I don't know, I guess maybe Lio's my new animal. And Sandwich, of course. And Zipper. I should make a picture book about us or something. Two teenage boys and two animals—this is the 2002 version of the blended family.

I can't believe I'm thinking of him as a familial candidate. I mean, come on, I barely know the kid. What do we even do together? Sometimes we go skateboarding because, I don't know, I guess we think we're eleven. He smokes clove cigarettes and I pretend I don't hate the smell. We drink Slurpees and . . . we do stuff like push each other on gates, I guess.

I wish I knew what was going on.

I really can't get into this right now. I probably shouldn't have kissed him back. But I've sort of wanted to kiss him ever since I saw his fucked-up hair that day in Ms. Hoole's class, and really since the conversation right after, when he told me he cuts it when he's nervous, and I immediately wanted to know everything in the whole world that makes him nervous, and everything in the whole world about him.

I should have invited him to stay tonight. He'd fit well into this silence at the dinner table. I think it's bad when I'm allowed to dwell in my head for this long. Someone should be dragging me out into conversation, but usually it's someone on TV and tonight there's no TV.

It's not that we don't get along—my parents and my brother and me—it's that we don't have a whole lot in common, and we all have these different ideas of how to use this house and this family. My dad wants a house full of books and rousing dinner-table discussions about whether or not Lolita was a slut. My mom is already talking about arranging a Secret Santa thing among the four of us, won't that be fun? My brother wants this to be his airport, his temporary base in all his running around, complete with full-service restaurant and four-dollar massages, and he'll pay for us by the hour, no problem, if we will just treat him as well as he deserves. But we never do, even I know that.

And I want something to take care of.

We listen to Dad squeak his knife around for a minute. It's brutal. Todd clears his throat, then he stands up and turns on the radio. He plunks it down in the center of the table like it's something for us to eat.

My father sighs, a little.

Todd tunes the radio to a news station and settles back into his green beans. The radio switches from weather to local news. A few car accidents, a stabbing, and two shootings, both in Glenmont. One was through the window of this craft store, Michael's, about a quarter mile from the

Glenmont metro. The bullet didn't hit anyone. An hour later and two miles away, a bullet did—someone in the parking lot of the Shopper's Food Warehouse. He's dead.

My father shakes his head while he drinks.

"Weird it made the news," Todd said. "People get shot all the time."

My father says, "Not while they're shopping," which is pretty representative of his world view. My dad's old enough that even September 11th didn't change his mind that violence only happens to violent people. The only people who get stabbed are in gangs. The only people who get shot, shot someone else first. As much as my bleeding heart wants to convince him this is wrong, the truth is most of the violence here *is* revenge-driven or gang-related. I should know, I mean, I go to public school.

The first shooting was at 5:20. That was when Lio kissed me, that was the exact minute. I know because I checked my watch afterward because I wanted to see how long it lasted, then I realized I hadn't checked my watch before he kissed me, so I'd never know. But I don't think it was very long, really.

No one died in the 5:20 shooting, which would have been kind of crazy romantic in this horrible way, and it would have given me an excuse to call him. But I don't think he would like the symbolism of "so, we're just a like a bullet that didn't hit anybody" any more than I do.

God, I hope he wouldn't like it any more than I do.

My mom finishes her dinner and stands up. "Ready, Craig?"

I say "Yeah," and pull on my jacket. I hope I don't get shot. That's pretty weird. I've never thought anything like that before. That kiss has me all screwed up.

We swing our flashlights back and forth, whistling and calling out names. Mom checks behind bushes and under the railing of the walkway to the metro. There's a couple making out on the bridge above us. I think it's one boy and one girl. Todd swears that he saw two homeless people having sex up there once—one boy and one girl.

"There are a lot of frogs here," I say. "We could get a frog."

She laughs in this way that says she doesn't know if I'm kidding.

"I only go for the fuzzy ones," I tell her.

"All right."

I take my comment out of context in my head and giggle a little. I only go for the fuzzy ones. Heh. This is a gross thing to be laughing about in front of your mom.

She's wearing the brown patchwork jacket I got her a million Christmases ago. She blows on her hands and runs them through her hair. "I hope we find Casablanca," she says. "She's my favorite." Casablanca is a Labrador retriever. She's old and missing a leg.

"We'll find her," I say. "She's easy. Easy to describe in posters and stuff. Easy to hear coming."

But the cold is making my nose run and making it a little hard to breathe, and right now nothing sounds very easy.

I wipe my nose.

Mom flicks her flashlight beam to me, and I look away quickly. "It's cold," I say stupidly, and crunch some of the leaves on the ground. It's not like she'd get upset if I were crying. I cry like three times a day, so it's the opposite of a big deal. It'd be like getting concerned every time I eat a meal.

Mom says, "I called the shelter this morning. They have all their descriptions, and they're all looking out, just waiting for someone to bring them in."

"Okay."

She says, "I'm so sorry this happened, sweetheart."

"We're going to find them. We're going to find all of them. That's right, yeah?"

"Yes." Mom cups her hand around the back of my head. "That's right."

I felt better when Lio comforted me, but it's still nice to be here for a minute, with Mom, searching for animals that she never even wanted.

We find Jupiter, who's this amazing Chihuahua-pug mix, trying to pick a fight with some bigger dogs a few blocks away. We start to head home with him, and my heart is pounding against his little body, and then we find Caramel, and just when everything feels so, so amazing, we find my parakeet, Fernando, except he's dead.

It's like a punch in the chest.

But Caramel and Jupiter scurry out of my arms as soon as we're home and go rub up against the couch and chew on the rug, and everything feels a little more possible again.

I leave them for a minute to go outside. I make a cross out of sticks and scratch Fernando's name in the dirt, then I cross it out and write Flamingo instead. He would have liked that.

But he isn't buried here. I didn't move his body from where we found it by the side of the road. I was too scared. I didn't want to touch it. I suck.

We're still missing:

Three dogs.

Three cats.

Three rabbits.

A guinea pig.

I close my eyes and listen to the animals inside my head and the memory of his chirping and the silence all the way around me.

LIO

CRAIG IS THE ROCK IN MY PROVERBIAL SHOE.

He's completely unavailable. He told me himself.

"I'm like sold-out movie tickets, is what I am," he once said. "I'm, like, at that same level, is the thing, and I'm not saying you would care or anything, but just in case like, that friend of yours wanted to hit on me or something, you should maybe just let her know that I'm completely unavailable. And gay, but that would be like such a lesser problem than how unavailable I am, because I am *that* unavailable."

And then he sticks himself right onto my life. And onto my mind. He is unavailable and inescapable.

A while ago, he had this boyfriend. Cody. Stuff didn't

work out. I have a feeling the guy treated Craig like shit, but I don't know details.

But now Craig isn't open to affection from anything that doesn't have fur. This explains why, even after an afternoon looking for his animals, I'm home instead of with him. He didn't ask me to stay. It doesn't explain why I kissed him.

I guess his face explains why I kissed him. I'm weak.

And I like that he wants me to talk. I'm not really going to talk. It's nothing personal, and it's not deep or exciting. It's just something I don't do.

But he wants me to. There's something interesting about the way he wants me to, because his reasons are different from my family's and my teachers' and my therapist's. They want to know that I'm normal. When I talk, they feel better.

Craig wants to know what I have to say.

I wish he knew that, the truth is, I don't have much say. I'm not an enigma. I'm just talked out, probably permanently. I said all I needed to say when I was a boy made of sticks and radiation and half-digested oatmeal. *I don't feel good. I want to go home. Make it stop.* It's been seven years, and I'm still out of words.

Kissing him also probably has something to do with the fact that I'm so bored that I either want to die or jump on the next plane home.

My sister Jasper says, "Weren't you in Glenmont today?"

I don't know how she knows this. Maybe she analyzed the gravel samples from my sneakers.

I shrug and turn back to my computer. I'm trying to write an email. It's really irritating emailing with Craig, because he responds a few seconds after I hit send. It's gratifying, but problematic, as it takes me an hour to write a few witty paragraphs.

And what do I say to him now? How am I even supposed to explain?

Craigy—

Funny story, I saw a little chocolate on your lips and realized I was ravenously hungry. Sorry for attacking your face.

Hell no.

"Two people were shot in Glenmont today," she says.

Sometimes it's like Jasper never lived in New York.

And I saw the news too. One person got shot, and one store full of people watched a bullet glide harmlessly onto the floor. Jasper wants to be a writer, and she can't even get her facts straight.

She sighs. "Come on. I'm taking you to therapy tonight."

I make a face because it's my duty to, as her little brother, but the truth is I don't mind Jasper all that much. Growing up, we used to have all these family talent shows, and

Jasper and I always won. We were the true rock stars of the family, since my twin brother, Theodore—yeah, Theo and Lio, it's a problem—preferred being in the audience. The rest of our sisters were too young or too old to qualify for our fantasy band. I can sing, and Jasper knows how to shred an air guitar.

Theodore never participated in the talent shows. He was a whiny kid and always said he wasn't feeling good enough, even though I would be up there singing my heart out in front of the fireplace, if it was a good week, or on top of my hospital bed, if it wasn't. I sang even more as I got well, which is something else Theo never did.

He's the reason I'm in therapy. My mother's abandonment and the cancer as a whole and September 11th also have something to do it with, but Theo is the reason everyone knows I need therapy. Theo is the reason I don't like to talk.

There isn't some long, drawn-out, tortured explanation. It's really pretty basic.

My brother and I had the same face.

My brother and I had the same voice.

For some reason, he was born to talk and I was born to sing. We always knew that.

For some reason, we both got cancer.

For some reason, here I am.

Yaaay therapy. I've been in it for seven years. That's

almost half my life, and longer than any human has any excuse to be in therapy. It's a testament, at the very least, to the longevity of my . . . something. Whatever it is that's wrong with me. Not cancer.

When we decided we were moving, no one even considered *not* finding me a new therapist. It was a priority nearly as high as finding a place to live.

"You're a little fucked up, aren't you?" this therapist said in our first meeting, after she'd finished reading through my file. She'd skimmed it already, she said, but she read through it twice again while I sat there, since it was probably clear I didn't have much to say. She then told me I was a little fucked up, and I decided I liked her.

Her name is Adelle. We've been meeting for two months now, so, in therapist-time, we're basically best friends. She's not so hard to talk to, probably because I know she can't get bored of me and walk away. She doesn't care that there isn't much to me. She still gets paid.

So today I tell her about Craig, and looking for the animals, and kissing him. She says she didn't know I was gay. I say that's pretty stupid, since I've definitely mentioned my Gerard Butler dreams, and did she think those were purely metaphorical?

"I was practically there when that man got shot," I say.

"Really. In Glenmont today?"

"Yeah."

"Interesting," she says, and then doesn't speak for a minute. "So, do you feel like you escaped something?"

"Not really. Why would someone kill me?"

"I don't know," she says, in this way like she's leading me, but what else am I supposed to feel? I'm not going to walk around worrying that someone's going to shoot me.

She lets us sit there in silence for a minute. Then she says, "So how do you feel about kissing Craig?"

I chew on my fingernails. No words are coming to me.

"Are you interested in him?" she asks.

This is a euphemism. *Do you* like *him?* was the euphemism in grade school. Now it's *Are you interested in him?*

I'm interested in Craig because Craig is interesting. He'll talk forever, and he never worries about saying something stupid. I once heard him have an entire conversation with himself about whether he should bring his biology book to history or come back and grab it between classes. He didn't know I was listening, but once he realized I was there, he wasn't embarrassed. He went right back into his conversation, his head, his world. Seriously, five minutes on whether to bring his biology book.

He's unscared and he's interesting. He has a menagerie and funny clothes and a good sense of humor.

That's not what Adelle wants to know. She wants to know if I'm *interested* in Craig.

I shrug. *Yes.*

I *like* him.

I want to share my lunch with him. As long as we're talking grade school, this is how I feel.

Back when we used to IM all the time, before I met him, he told me this, in a series of messages—**so just so you know, im not really a fifty-eight-year-old fat guy or anything, but i thought you should know, in case my appearance was of any consequence to you, that im not exceptionally gorgeous or anything and i really couldnt win *people*'s sexiest man alive, no matter what that cashier at the supermarket said. youre probably straight, so i doubt this is real important to you, but i kinda thought you should know, just in case you thought the school chose me as an ambassador for my eight-pack or golden blond hair or something.**

So I said *okay*. But then I saw him. His hair might not be golden blond—he's black, so that would be a little weird—but his eyes kind of are. That zip-up red hoodie he wears makes him look like he just got back from apple picking. And God I need to shut up because I might be growing a vagina.

Adelle says, "Lio?"

"I'm listening," I say. But she isn't saying anything.

She laughs a little. "That's not exactly how this is supposed to work."

Sometimes I hate therapy.

I pick up the Play-Doh and start building a snowman.

Therapist's offices always come equipped with things to do besides pay attention.

"Looking forward to the holidays?" she asks, watching me.

That's sort of a stretch. Snowmen are really easy to make out of Play-Doh. "I'm Jewish."

"I didn't say Christmas."

That's true. Damn.

"I don't care," I say.

This is a bad session, and it's my fault. I try very hard to use my therapy time well. That's why it's all the more depressing that I still need it.

Get better. Get better. Everyone wants you to get better.

"Do you want to talk about the shootings?" Adelle asks.

"Two random shootings."

"If you think they're stupid, why did you bring them up?"

"Thought you'd be interested."

"Why?"

I pull my snowman into pieces. "It's the kind of thing people always care about. I almost had a near-death experience."

"And?"

She has me talking and she knows it.

I say. "Almost having a near-death experience is the next best thing to actually having one. If you want to be interesting."

"And having a near-death experience is the next best thing to actually dying?"

I shrug.

Adelle makes a note on her pad. It looks like a check mark. She says, "So do you feel like it was a near-death experience?"

What? "No." I step on my shoelace and pull it out of its bow. "But . . ."

"Talk."

"Just . . . I didn't almost die in nine eleven."

"Yes?"

"Neither did my friends. But . . . for a long time, we kept comparing. Who was closer to almost dying. Closer to the towers. Trying to beat each other."

"And you didn't like that?"

"Proximity isn't a merit badge. It doesn't actually mean anything." I put my snowman back together. This time, I give him a hat.

I waste our last five minutes by thinking about Craig instead of talking. Eventually, Adelle says, "Okay, Lio. I'll see you on Friday."

CRAIG

I COME IN FROM FLAMINGO'S NOT-QUITE FUNERAL, and I spend so much time hugging the animals that it takes me a while to check my email, which is weird, because it's usually the first thing I do, and then the second thing, and then the third, refresh refresh refresh.

I got an email from Lio. I don't think I'd know anything about Lio if not for emails and those IMs. But I'm not sure how much he would mean to me if all I saw was the confident, kind of douchey boy who writes these emails and IMs, as much as I like that boy. I don't know how all the parts of Lio manage to mash up and work for me, but somehow it happens. Somehow the bits and pieces of him keep coming together in my head again and again, like when you watch *The Wizard of Oz* while playing *The Dark Side of the Moon,* and somehow it all fits together. Even though it's probably not supposed to.

Anyway, I got this email.

Craig—

Hope your house is a little noisier already. Let me know if you need to borrow a TV. My sister Veronica's set is still here in some box. She's too holistic for it now, or something.

But really, I hope it's louder because there are more animals.

Went to therapy. You'll be happy to know I'm still a little fucked up. We didn't talk about DEAD BROTHER this session. Kind of a gyp. Veronica would hit me if she knew I said gyp.

Can I be honest with you? I like talking about DEAD BROTHER with you a lot more than I like talking about him with thera thera therapist (that's her full name). So if you want to talk about it or whatever? If you ever need a reason to feel depressed or you want to feel thankful for your lymphocytes or whatever, yeah, I can hook you up.

I liked that shirt you wore today.

We can talk about me getting all cougar (you're more than six months younger than me, you know) on you if you want. Or we can pretend that it's just that thing where two gay boys kiss because they're the only two gay boys around. Like on sitcoms. And then we adopt a Vietnamese baby.

I'm not delusional enough to think this is a sitcom. It's not like I have wedding bands picked out or something.

See you tomorrow.

Lio

I'm not sure I can deal with this tonight. The self-awareness of it is kind of killing me—how many times did Lio edit this email? It's so fucking carefully constructed, and that's not the kind of thing I can handle, so I always just reply as fast as I can without thinking and right now I'm just so tired.

And the part about his brother is the worst, because I'd totally talk to him about it, I'd love to talk to him about it, I live to drink up other people's problems and pee them out and probably drink them again, knowing me, though it's not like that turns me on or whatever, but if it did I'd know just the websites because insomnia is ridiculous.

But anyway, no matter how many times Lio says "Yeah,

we'll talk," the bottom line is, the kid doesn't talk, and I want him to, because I'd like to see what he says when he doesn't edit. I want to see if it's beautiful, because right now I don't know.

Or we could . . . use our mouths for other things, is I guess what I'm trying to say. I mean, if that's easier for him. Or if it's even possible for me, in my current state of eunuch.

God, I'm so tired, and I don't know what I want, which is probably why kissing seems like the best option, but it sounds like he doesn't even want to kiss me anymore, so now I don't even know. I should go to sleep, I guess.

I check the kennels and the beds again and again, and I pet Caramel for ages until he starts to get really annoyed with me. I should sleep.

That's my part of me that's "a little fucked up," I guess. If we can divide ourselves up that way. I have Cody and the fact that I don't sleep. And the animals, though I guess they're all connected or some shit like that. God, I should go to therapy with Lio. I bet she'd have a field day between the two of us. And then we'd get better, because I guess that's the point of therapy, and then what? And what happens when you don't get better? I know the answer to that and it's not something I want to happen to me. Or Lio. Although I guess he probably knows more than I do about not getting better, but the more I get to know Lio, the more I learn that you can't use cancer as a metaphor for real life.

I flop down on my couch and turn on the TV. Sandwich walks in a circle on my back like a dog before she settles down. I hear my parents walking around upstairs, shutting off the lights and double-checking all the locks on the doors before they go to bed. The windows are already fixed, because it's not safe to have all that broken glass around when there are animals.

I can hear my brother getting ready for the suicide hotline job. He likes it, even though the pay is shitty and it's about people killing themselves. He says he likes to help. My family is all full of beautiful people who care about everyone they don't know, and then we can't even get along most of the time. I think it's gotten to the extent that, if we were going to kill ourselves, none of us would think to call my brother for help first, and isn't that just the most pathetic thing in the whole world?

The man on the TV talks about a big jigsaw puzzle I can buy for four payments of something—no, three payments of something, special TV offer, I need to call right now. I don't even have a phone with me. I am a waste of his infomercial. There's no way he could make money off of me, and I feel really guilty about that.

Also, I sort of don't understand TV, in that way. Why do ratings matter? Do people get money when I watch their show? What about when I turn a show off in the middle? I guess I'm not part of that eighteen-to-thirty-five age group, or whatever it is everyone gives a shit about, so it probably doesn't matter. I barely matter, if you're looking at numbers—what's a fifteen-year-old? I can't even drive. And I'm six months younger than Lio.

I don't feel six months younger than Lio. I mean, I can deal with my life and stuff. And I've had a boyfriend and Lio hasn't, as far as I know. Or a girlfriend. So really, I'm older in a lot of ways.

I should sleep. It's been quiet upstairs for ages. I was a wreck in school today. Nearly started crying in algebra just because I couldn't figure out the next step in this proof, which is really unacceptable behavior. I was falling asleep all through history, and now I'm awake like someone's electroshocked me.

Cody was older than me too. Nearly a year. Cody Cody Cody. Why didn't I get an email from him tonight? Usually he emails every night. Every single night, around nine o'clock. And I respond faster than I can breathe.

He didn't email tonight, for the first time since he's been gone. I'm trying to act like this is something I've just realized while I've been lying here watching the infomercial, acting like it hasn't been chewing on my thoughts ever since I checked my email and it was only Lio. Pretending there's this vague possibility that Cody wasn't the first thing I thought about for once.

Damn it.

I drag my laptop in front of the TV and boot up an old email from him, from a few weeks ago.

Craig—

To die by your side, baby. I heard that song today and it reminded me of

I mean

Still mad at you. Mad at you forever. Fuck you, Craig, fuck you and everything you did.

Love,
C

He's sent me over a hundred emails, and every single one contains, in some form, usually more than one form, the phrase, *Fuck you, Craig.*

And I email him back like my life depends on it. Every. Single. Time.

Because every email he sends has the word "love," too.

But today no email, so am I supposed to email him anyway? I don't know what to say. Usually I respond to him. Usually I only email because I need to know that he's okay.

I never tell him anything real. I don't want to weigh him down with stuff from here.

"I miss you I miss you I miss you," I whisper and stupid Sandwich thinks I'm talking to her and stretches her paws all the way out, and her claws come out and dig into my head a little, and damn it, Sandwich, I love you, but this is about Cody.

I want to email him, but if I do I'll stay up until he answers, I'll stay up worrying, I'll stay up freaking out that he's hurt and wonder why he isn't screaming at me with capital letters from my inbox. I'll spend every second I don't sleep pouring all of me into that computer, and I have animals to feed, animals to look for, animals to pet and hold and love me.

So I sleep a little, and my alarm goes off at five thirty, and I feed the animals, which takes about thirty seconds because there are not nearly enough, but by the time I get to school this girl Caitlin, who only wakes up ten minutes before school starts and brags about it and looks like it, is all, "Did you hear there was another shooting?" in her un-toothbrushed voice.

I say, "Yeah? Shocking," which is pretty douchey of me, but, seriously? Someone got shot in the world and now this is like the fucking Berlin Wall or some other shit people care about.

"This guy in Kensington. He was mowing his lawn. My dad was mowing the lawn yesterday! I mean, Jesus, it makes you think."

I don't see Lio until after second period. Some days I go most of the morning without seeing him, since we don't have any classes together until third period, but usually one of us seeks the other one out. It's nine thirty, and two more people have been shot since I talked to Caitlin. A few people are talking about it, but the news isn't sweeping the school like wildfire or anything. I heard two of the student teachers discussing it, or I wouldn't know.

It's four dead people. I don't mean to sound like that doesn't suck. I mean, obviously people shouldn't get shot. But this isn't God Bless America anymore, and things happen, people get shot.

Lio has a pink armband on, like now that he's kissed me he's fine with the whole world finding out he's gay. Though I don't know if anyone else would notice the armband, since it kind of goes with his usual quirky attire, and I don't know if he was ever in the closet to begin with or if he didn't advertise it because he's one of those people who thinks it's only your business if his cock is in your mouth. Maybe he's bi. Or maybe he's one of those guys who thinks that just because he likes guys doesn't mean he has to be part of some community. I don't like those guys, to be honest, but that's really just because I love community.

The rest of him is mostly in black, like usual. He says he wears eyeliner on Halloween but only then. Once I had a wet dream about helping him put it on. I can't believe I'm thinking about this right now.

"Maybe this is the apocalypse," I suggest to Lio, instead of "hello" or "thanks for last night" or "what made you think you could do that, but again maybe?" Or "no."

He raises his eyebrows at me.

If we're not going to talk about the kiss, are we at least going to talk about the email that talked about talking about the kiss? Correction—am *I* going to talk about the email? Because it's not like he will. And no. I'm not.

I say, "You know that whole thing about the world ending with a whimper, not a bang? This is actually how it's going to happen. We get shot until there's no one left."

I touch his hand because I'm dying to, all of a sudden. Just a tap with my finger on his palm.

He says, point-blank, "That's awful."

"Well, we'd last for a long time, I think. I get the feeling we'd be resourceful and everything." I clear my throat and take my hand away. "I was just joking around."

"Yeah." He slings his backpack over his shoulder like he's about to leave, but he doesn't move. He's staring me down, or up, I guess, because he has to tilt his chin at a pretty wide angle to look at me. And he's still fierce and frightening.

But I'm angry. "Maybe I'm scared," I say. "Maybe I'm scared and deflecting."

"Maybe."

"Did you consider that?"

He shrugs.

"I mean, Jesus, Lio." What am I so mad at him about? I lean against his locker. "I mean . . . I could be scared." I could be a lot of things and he fucking wouldn't know, maybe that's the point.

He starts walking to his next class, or to somewhere, or maybe just to anywhere that's not here. I jog beside him. He used to run cross-country, and those short legs know how to move.

He says, "You're not."

"I'm not what?"

"Scared."

"Three random people—"

"Four."

"—have been shot. I completely have a right to be scared. I could be quaking in my boots. Sneakers."

"You're complacent," he says.

A three-syllable word from Lio is enough cause to stop walking, so I do, and he comes to rest beside me. But I can tell he really doesn't want to stop walking, and he doesn't want to look at me, and he certainly doesn't want to talk to me.

At least not about people dying.

Wait, so which one of us is the coward here? Because I would rather talk about people getting shot than talk about him kissing me, and how pathetic is that? Right now I want to crawl back in bed rather than talk about anything real. It's so much easier to debate and argue over this shit that has nothing to do with us or how we feel. Random people that happen to die in our random city.

I say, "I'm not . . . complacent."

"You don't think you're going to get shot."

I rub the back of my neck. "Well, yeah. I mean, chances are, I'm not going to get shot."

"You're right."

I look at him.

Lio's really into numbers. He counts when he's nervous. I'll put my hand on his back, and he'll give me this really small smile—*sorry. I'm a little fucked up.*

He sighs. "You think you won't get shot because you're you. *You* doesn't get shot. Won't happen to *you.*"

I catch my breath. "So?"

"It's bullshit." He shrugs.

"You can't pretend like I should be out there fearing for my life. Come on. The odds are . . . I mean, four people? Odds were pretty good that none of those would be me, you know that. If we're playing the odds . . ."

"Be confident because the odds are in your favor." He

clears his throat, like talking this much hurts him. "Not because you're a special snowflake."

This isn't fair. None of this is fair.

I don't know if I'm special, but yeah, there's that heartbeat telling me, *I'm Craig, I'm Craig,* and I don't think I need to apologize for that. I'm Craig, and Craig is alive. I know that. It's basically the first thing I know when I get up in the morning, so yeah, I'm not really open to the idea of that changing any more than I'm open to the idea that I'll stand up and there won't be floor. Is that a problem? I can't be the only one who feels this way. I think that's consciousness, and I think it might be the thing that keeps me from being a sociopath.

"You won't get shot," he says. "It's a numbers game."

Right now my heartbeat's all out of whack trying to thrum out, *Why did you kiss me and why won't you do it again?* But I can't ask it, I can't.

Anyway, by the time we get out of class, someone else has been killed. A twenty-five-year-old woman was pumping gas, and someone shot her in the head. At long range, like all the others.

I'm so mad. I'm just mad about everything. I feel like this proves Lio right or wrong but I don't even know what his damn point is, and in fifth period he barely even looks at me. He just sits there and doodles a lot.

× × ×

Mom picks me up after school and there's Kremlin in the backseat, pounding her paws against the leather, and I cuddle that dog so hard that I'm worried I'm going to rub all her fur off or something, and she licks my face over and over, and she smells funny but I don't even care.

"The lady who found her was excited to get rid of her, I think," Mom says. "God, she's a loud one. I think your dad would have preferred she stayed lost."

I cover Kremlin's ears.

Usually, when I take one of the pets out somewhere by himself—like to the vet, or maybe if he's been sad, out on a special walk—we're greeted by a whole host of jealous, curious animals as soon as we come back through the front door. It's weird when only Jupiter and the two cats run up to sniff Kremlin's legs. It makes it very hard to be happy, when I think that tonight I will be walking so many fewer dogs than I am supposed to.

Then Todd comes down from upstairs and gives me this huge hug. I say, "Hey," because this is a little weird.

"I'm glad you're okay," he says.

It's like no one would have told him if I'd died at school or something. I say, "What?"

"You didn't hear about the shootings?"

"Oh, right, I mean, I heard about them, but I wasn't thinking about them or something." I want to tell him that the chances are way better that I'd died in a car wreck with Mom on the way home, but I don't mind when Todd likes me, even though I sometimes feel like I'm just his good deed for the day.

Dad finally comes home with a stack of papers, rubbing the headache between his eyes. Parents are calling him like crazy, he says, all of them demanding that he promise their kids will be safe, like that's something Dad can tell them.

We eat a late dinner, and I should do my homework but I don't, and I should sleep but I don't, and while we're sitting around chewing on our cold, gummy pizza, a man is killed crossing the street in Washington, D.C. Wha-pam, long-range bullet, dead body.

I email the boy I shouldn't instead of the boy I should. Because there is nothing from Cody in my inbox. Nothing, nothing, nothing.

Lio—

I don't know why you have to be a jackass all the time. It didn't used to be like this.

Craig

Craig—

We didn't used to know each other. I'm a jackass sometimes. It's not really all the time. You'll deal.

Lio

———————————

Lio—

I wish you would call me.

I wish you talked.

You don't think anyone's going to shoot an animal, right?

Craiger

God, the least Lio could do is answer this one, let me know that the animals are safe, even though why do I trust him to know when I don't trust my dad to know about his students? The animals aren't Lio's job. They have nothing to do with Lio.

LIO

I'M ABOUT TO ANSWER CRAIG'S EMAIL WHEN DAD comes in. He wants to chat. That's sort of his thing. Our thing. Though my part is mostly listening.

I'm his only son. It's stupid to say we have a special bond just because of that, but we do, I think. I think I'm a relief for him, like an oasis among all the girls. We sit and watch football together. I haven't told him I'm gay, but he's probably figured it out. If he hasn't, I don't think it's going to be a big deal to him, as long as I assure him we can still watch football.

In a way, my role for him has changed. Now most of the girls are gone, since Mom left and the big girls are at college. The single-parent situation, even with only three kids here, is hard for Dad. These things mean that I feel now like less of a respite for Dad and more like just another person bearing down on him. So I have to use that bond to our advantage.

Music comes pouring in as soon as Dad opens the door, because my little sister, Michelle, is watching MTV in the living room. My dad shuts the door and the noise blurs out. I don't know why he doesn't tell her to turn it down or watch TV that has people wearing clothes.

"Hey, Lio."

I smile at him.

"How's school?" he asks me. He peeks under my hat and laughs a little. "Look at your hair."

"Sorry."

"Don't apologize to me. You're the one who has to walk around like that."

"School's fine."

"Good to hear." He aims his gaze toward the living room. "I think Michelle's having a rough time making friends."

That doesn't make much sense. Michelle is bubbly. She and Jasper both—though Jasper had issues at her last school because of some boy dating her and this other girl at once. So she was excited to move. Michelle was apathetic, I think.

"She misses New York, I think," Dad says. My dad has the collar of his shirt unbuttoned and his tie loose around his neck. He's gained too much weight. His stomach's hiding his belt buckle, and I can see his shoulders move when he breathes, just from climbing the two flights of stairs to our apartment. "But at least Jasper's happy, and God knows that's a victory worth celebrating. Did you go jogging today?"

I nod. Jogging and singing are my two favorite things, but singing doesn't make a good recreational activity unless you like being annoying. Which I do not.

"How far?" he asks me.

"Five miles," I say.

"And how fast?"

I like when Dad leads me. I hate when anyone else does. "Thirty-nine minutes."

"Way to go, kid." He puts his hand on top of my hat. His hand is so big that he could palm my skull like a basketball and lift it right off my shoulders. He could tuck it under his arm and bring me with him everywhere.

"I miss New York," I say. The moment felt right somehow.

He looks at me, his eyes suddenly soft. These are the moments I love best with my dad. When I stop being his boy and I can just be his kid. We stop acting like *men*. That's the special part. I think the girls are always his girls.

He says, "You do?"

I nod.

I miss feeling strong and defiant. There's something

about being a NYC native that means you have a lot less to prove.

Dad says, "Was the anniversary hard for you?"

There are a lot of anniversaries he could mean. His and Mom's, their third since they separated, was last week. My sisters and I took him out for dinner but didn't talk about it. I think that was exactly what he wanted.

My no-more-chemo thing was actually yesterday, but I think Dad probably forgot about that. It's a stupid thing to celebrate. My brother died on March 8th, and we always visit his grave and the children's hospital, and that serves as the day we think about how glad we are that the cancer's gone.

So I know what anniversary he means.

"No one here understands," I say.

Dad says, "They had the Pentagon."

I shrug. It's not the same.

It's numbers. Just like chances are Craig isn't going to get shot, the chances are that if someone died in September 11th, they died in New York, not in Washington, D.C. It's just numbers.

It makes sense, then, that the way they memorialized it at school wasn't nearly the production I was expecting. We had a candle-lighting ceremony. The chorus sang a few songs. We missed one period for the assembly, then we trotted on back to class. All I really felt was a nagging feeling I should have signed up for chorus.

I wanted to email a friend back home and ask what it was like at my old school, but I didn't know how to ask in a way that wouldn't seem . . . vulgar. *So, how was your September 11th?*

Jasper calls, "Dad?" from the kitchen, so he smiles at me and gets up. "We'll talk more later," he says. "I'm glad you're doing okay, Li."

I wonder where he got the impression that I'm doing okay, but actually, I am.

Well, I'm not great or anything, but I'm probably not getting any worse.

Craigy—

Dad and I just had a nice talk about STATISTICS. Facts and figures and such. You know how fathers are. Did yours make you memorize baseball cards?

Washington DC didn't come off looking so hot.

But you always do.

I can't send that.
He'd probably be offended.
Or aroused.
And neither of those is really my intention.

Probably.

I hold down backspace.

I should probably make some cancer-kid joke. Those always go over well with Craig. I can't decide if this is a horrible idea, since I snarked at him for making fun of dead people earlier today.

Generally, I can't decide if I should feel ashamed about the cancer jokes.

Leukemia, after all the Lifetime movies, begs to be made fun of. It's so overinflated. Plus it's been seven years, so at this point, it really does feel like a joke. Like a gross-out story someone told me when I was a kid.

I could say that with full confidence if I didn't still sometimes wake up from nightmares that make me breathe so hard I throw up. But they are less and less frequent every year.

Cancer is just a way to be sick in real life, but in movies and stuff it's shorthand for *he was young and beautiful and pure and then he got sick and he suffered and he had poignant last words and he died.* And I can tell myself that's what happened with Theodore, though it's not entirely accurate. His last word was "water" and he died before he could drink it. You can make that beautiful, if you want. But the reality is, he was a thirsty forty-pound boy, and he died whining.

And the beautiful tragic death is obviously not how it worked out for me. So, way to fuck up, leukemia.

But the idea that this shitty disease sanctified our lives really bothers me. I wasn't *brave*. I wasn't a *fighter*. I was the one who responded to Jasper's marrow transplant. I was a statistic. And so was Theo.

The bottom line is, cancer happens the exact same way other things happen: It does, or it doesn't. But it never means anything.

Okay, cool, but this isn't writing my email to Craig. And, hey, guess what? This isn't about Theo.

Craigy—

Sorry about all the bad stuff.

Be well.

Lio

PS Your animals are safe. Promise.

I hit send before I can stop myself.

CRAIG

I CAN'T SLEEP. I WRITE EMAILS.

I can't believe I'm writing to Cody. That after all of that bullshit and mindfucking I put myself through about not writing to Cody before he emailed me, now I'm doing it. It's his turn. The way I was supposed to keep from going crazy was I was going to only email when it was my turn, because then I wasn't crazy, then I wasn't needy, I was just being polite, I was just being fair, it was *my* choice whether or not to respond, mine. And here I am writing back to an email he never sent. I'm writing to him because he's ignoring me.

I knew it. I knew all along that I would keep
coming
back.
I'm that boy.

C—

Didn't hear from you today, Cody. You doing okay? How's school?

Things are okay here.

I pause and stare at what I've written. Well. I'm clearly the
fucking master of conversation. I should teach lessons or
something. Lio could pay me a hundred fucking dollars a
week to learn to perform that kind of brilliant wordsmith-
ing I demonstrated right there.

I keep typing. If I stop to think, that's when I start crying
or otherwise get fucked.

My animals escaped. We've found some—remember Sandwich?
and Kremlin? I sent you pictures, you remember—and it's hard
and kind of scary. No one is giving up, so pray for them, okay?
Hey, I wanted to apologize for always making fun of you when you
prayed. Really, I thought it was cute the whole time, I just thought
you liked being teased, I don't know. I'm stupid. But it helped me
sleep when you wished that I would. I mean prayed that I would.

I hope school's going okay. Did you get into that art class after all? I'll come up there and bash some skulls together or something if you need. If that would help.

I ran into your mother at the grocery store the other day. She had a bag of avocados, said she'd tell you hi from me next time you called, but I said she didn't need to because you were still emailing, but I kind of hope she said hi for me anyway. Also, are we still emailing?

Love,
C

I put my head down next to my keyboard. Kremlin wants to know what's wrong.

"I have a broken heart," I tell her.

She whines a little.

I say, "Yeah, I know. I don't like it either."

Cody . . .

I've known Cody since I was six. We used to play together because we lived next door as toddlers, and even though he moved away before we were really aware of each other, our moms stayed friends so we saw each other a lot for those forced play dates, and eventually we begged for play dates every day. We were the exact same height when I was in first grade—like, to the centimeter. We thought that was really cool. Of course, by the time we started hooking up, I was practically twice his size. But when I was six, we were perfectly matched and it was great.

I'm not huge, though I guess I must look really tall next to the boys I keep . . . doing things with. I'm tall enough that people always tell me I should play basketball (though when you're black, you only have to be like five foot ten before people start asking) but not the kind of freaky tall where I have to worry about how high doorways are. It's not really a big deal, so it's weird that it keeps being this thing that I think about, although usually I think about it in terms of Lio's smallness rather than my largeness, and maybe that means something, but probably not, because it has nothing to do with Cody.

Anyway, when Cody grew up, or I grew up and he stayed small, he turned into some kind of a big deal—a fantastic soccer player, a huge smile, a personality that seemed like it must have eaten bits of other people's to get that big, like a very hungry caterpillar. He was so much more than alive. He always was.

Our first kiss was in fourth grade for me and fifth grade for him, when we were playing hide-and-seek. I said if I found him in less than two minutes, I got to kiss him. I don't remember what happened if I didn't. But I found him in a minute and forty-two seconds, roughly, and he was inside this old chest that holds all these old clothes that my grandmother draped all over herself before she died, and I pulled him out of the chest and he was shrouded in turquoise and gold and I kissed him.

We waited until I turned fifteen because even we thought it was a little weird to have sex at fourteen, and he was sixteen and really not okay with having sex with a middle schooler, so that was the summer before ninth grade for me, and the summer before tenth grade for him, and he was almost sixteen, and that was our summer.

It was so ours, that whole summer.

It was awkward and difficult and painful at first, but he loved me and we were really gentle, and then it got good. Really good. It got closer to the movies than antiseptic health class told me it ever could.

So fuck health class and fuck the preachy advice your parents give you, because sex didn't ruin our relationship.

It's not that.

Although I can see, from an objective standpoint, that maybe I was too young, but is that really the point at all? Why the hell should I see things from an objective standpoint? I'm not objective, I mean, this is my life.

And if we stop having sex, the terrorists win, right?

I guess Lio would say that, statistically speaking, I was too young, since he's so crazy about numbers, and I'm sure that means that, from his perspective, I should have waited, because his whole fucking life is about how many other people are doing things. I'm sure he's a virgin. I'm sure he's waiting until he's exactly sixteen and seven months, which I think is the average age, but I think it's a lot higher for gay boys, eighteen or so, because it takes us longer to realize and find each other and, I don't know, wax off all our body hair or something.

But I didn't have to go through any of that with Cody because I guess we were made for each other and too young to have a lot of body hair.

He's a junior now. It's crazy to think about that, to think that actually right now, maybe he's thinking about college and SATs and stuff. Do they even talk about college at his school? Do kids from his school go to real college? Because it's not exactly a real school. I mean, it's called a school, a residential school, but it's pretty much a mental hospital with classes.

At least that's how I imagine it. It isn't like I've visited him, and is that the part that's important? That I haven't visited him, even though he's asked, he's said *fuck you fuck you Craig get up here goddamn it get here now,* and is it important that I haven't gone, or is it more important that that isn't a real invitation? Is it more important that Cody is there or that he's here in my head?

I think the part that's important is we kissed in my parents' attic when we were nine and ten.

That was great. And the summer before freshman year, the summer of 2001? That was a great summer. And then everything got so fucked up. I guess what happened is that the terrorists won.

My city, Silver Spring, isn't technically a city in the legal sense of the word, according to the internet. I'm not sure why. Downtown, where I almost, almost, am, looks like most small cities, in the way that it's a pretty rundown place, but with some tall buildings, and it has a general feeling of blue and brown. The streets are beautiful at night because of all the fast food places and the little liquor and wine stores. It looks like Christmas every night here, with all the brake lights and streetlights, and even along the highways, because you can see the lights from the hotels and churches. But on the edges of all of it, where the light almost, almost, but doesn't quite hit, the dark is very deep, darker than any of the places in the whole world that I've ever been.

These are the kinds of things you realize when you stare out your window all night, waiting for an email that doesn't come, listening to Sandwich whine for food even though there's still some in her bowl. I have this brutal headache, and I know I need to go to sleep, but right now sleep feels as impossible as holding my breath all night.

I wonder how many people are getting shot over these few hours. All over the world, how many people are getting shot tonight, in this weird time between October 3rd and October 4th?

It turns out, no one was shot, at least not in our area by a single long-range bullet, the news says this morning. But that's not even important, because the front page of the newspaper has an article tying all the shootings together, and there is, guaranteed, a sniper.

I read the word "sniper" and it's like a bell in my head, ringing and ringing with the realization that everything is about to get really weird.

My mom drops me off really close to the front door of my school, like I'm six or something. "Just to be safe," she says, and she gives me an extra kiss on each cheek. "I love you." She doesn't roll down the windows, even though it's not as cold outside as it has been and the leaves are falling and it already smells like Halloween. October has a smokier smell than September, like there are candles burning in pumpkins the whole month.

Before I get out of the car, she says, "Craig, maybe we should stop hunting for the animals for a while."

I look at her.

And my brain stops *CodyCodyCody*ing just long enough to think, *two dogs, three cats, three rabbits, one guinea pig.*

She says, "Okay, honey, I'm sorry. God, don't ever make

that face at me again." She hugs me, but I don't know what face I'm making, because I didn't mean to make a face. Maybe my normal face is just a really sad face, and how shitty would that be?

But the point is that I'm not going to stop looking for the animals, because they are mine and they are counting on me.

When I get out of the car, all these teachers and parent volunteers sweep in and form a pod around me until I reach the building. It's claustrophobic and annoying and I'm fifteen and I can take care of myself.

I'm doodling in American Civilizations when Mr. Spavich sets aside his lesson plan and says, "Okay. Do you want to talk about what's going on?"

We all look at him like we don't know what he's talking about.

"Are your parents afraid to pump gas?" he asks. "All of a sudden, that seems like a risky activity, doesn't it?"

We don't look at each other.

Mr. Spavich says, "Guys. It's okay to be scared."

Marisabel says, "If we're scared, the terrorists win. Isn't that what everyone said after September eleventh?"

"This isn't terrorists," Lio says under his breath. He's sitting next to me, wearing these fingerless gloves that make him look like a badass. After his email last night, I have no idea what to say to him. And I guess he's forgiven for kissing me, but I guess I still have that headache.

Dennis says, "Well, my parents are paying my brother to pump gas for them, which is kind of disgusting. Like, it's all well and good if he's the one who gets shot, we get it."

"There are articles online, now," Marisabel says. "Like, 'How Not To Get Shot While Pumping Gas.' People are getting paid to tell us how to not get randomly shot."

Lio writes *AND HOW DO YOU FEEL ABOUT THAT* in big letters on his notebook. Next to it is a scribble from his English class—*fucking Kafka climaxed too early*—that makes me smile. I chew my knuckle so I don't laugh, and he notices and gives me this fantastic grin, though I'm not sure he knows why I'm laughing, and I think that's okay. I think it's this thing that's okay, here in the middle of everything.

"Craig?" Mr. Spavich says.

Fuck. I look up.

He raises his eyebrows at me. "Thoughts?"

So I say my first thought. "I think it's really disrespectful and stupid to compare this to September eleventh."

Mr. Spavich says, "Oh?"

I bet American Civ had a field day last year, with September 11th. God, how can I even think things like that? I should be arrested. How many awful thoughts do you need to have before you count as a terrorist?

Lio whispers, "Numbers," but like he's talking to himself,

not to me. It's still enough for me to get my bearings.

I clear my throat. "Yeah. I mean . . . we *just* had the anniversary, and already we're looking for our next big tragedy? This doesn't compare at all. And how many people died in the Pentagon?"

"One hundred and eighty-nine," Mr. Spavich says.

Damn. That sounds so low. I thought it was more than that, and it throws me for a second, but then I remember what the Pentagon was and what this is and everything comes back faster and harder. I say, "But, yeah. A hundred and eighty-nine people versus six from a sniper? Like, a life is a life. . . ."

"And more lives is more lives," Mr. Spavich completes. He says this like it's my opinion, not his.

"Yes," Lio whispers, my stomach feels sick.

I say, "I guess so, yeah." My headache pulls and I realize that that isn't what I meant at all.

That isn't what made the Pentagon a bigger deal.

Because the reason I can't compare this to September 11th is that no one I know has been shot by the sniper. Maybe I only feel stuff if I'm holding hands with someone getting obliterated, or at the very least holding the hand of someone holding the hand of someone getting obliterated, and fuck, what does that say about my life?

Mr. Spavich asks who's been watching the news, and a few of us raise our hands, including this one boy who says he can't help watching the news because every time there's a shooting it interrupts regular programming for hours and hours. He's become an accidental rubbernecker. One girl says she isn't sleeping, and normally I'd roll my eyes at this, because I hate when people pull that, but, God, she looks like shit.

Her parents are telling her to run in zigzag patterns.

There's a boy wearing a camouflage jacket, and I guess it could be fashion statement, but I get the feeling it isn't, because he's tall and dark and stunning and I look at him a lot, but I've never seen that jacket before.

It's stupid, that jacket, so stupid. This isn't a jungle. This isn't a war zone.

LIO

CRAIG'S MOM ALWAYS PACKS HIM GOURMET LUNCHES.
She gives him a place mat for him to spread over his place
at the cafeteria. She doesn't know we eat outside every day,
I guess. We sit in the little field by the side of the school.
This time of year, it's more of a mud flat than a field, and
it's a little cold. But it's away from the noise.

I give him half of my peanut butter and jelly, and he
gives me half of his macaroni and cheese. It has pep-
pers and onions and something clear and spicy I don't
recognize.

We always eat lunch together. When he was home sick
two weeks ago, I hid in the library and shoveled down my

food as fast as I could. I don't know when I turned into such a freaky little loner.

There's an elementary school across the street. Craig's dad is the principal. Usually we watch the kids playing kickball and four-square. We pretend to be team captains and divvy up the eight-year-olds.

Today there's no one out.

The morning kindergarteners are heading toward the buses, but I can hardly see them. The teachers are forming a human cage.

"I watched *Bananas in Pyjamas* yesterday," Craig says.

I look at him.

He says, "Yeah, at like four in the morning. It reruns at weird times like that." Craig doesn't sleep. It bothers me.

"It was on some kids station and I got so sucked in," he says. "There is so much drama with those bananas. It's the Australians. They're sick, you know that? Sick and wrong and amazing. I love Australians. Best accents in the whole world. We should figure out how to do them and just do them all the time."

I smile at him.

He says, "Anyway, so I was reading some of our old IMs last night. Is that way too lame to admit? I mean, I was going through a ton of old emails."

I shake my head.

"And I was just thinking . . . I never would have guessed

you were this quiet. I mean, you told me you were shy, but I never would have really believed you if I hadn't met you, and actually seen that you're so . . . unresponsive."

That's not fair.

He says, "Online you were . . . you were kind of unreal. Like so big and personable as to be unreal. And I guess that's kind of the point. The 'un,' I mean. You were like so huge and confident and big and—"

"That's real."

"Hmm?"

And when I do talk, he doesn't listen. "This," I say. "That you noticed. That you're here regardless. That's the real part."

"Yeah, but where's *your* real part, okay? Because . . . because, here's the thing, what I need to know is . . . what part of this is real for me?"

"I don't like to talk."

"Yeah, I know. I'm pretty sure I've figured that out."

"But I like you."

He nods a little, not looking at me. I know. He's not ready. I'm pushing too hard. I kissed him and he didn't ask me out. Shouldn't that be the only signal I need? It's not like I don't know he's still hung up on his ex. Whatever. I can try not to care.

I should apologize for kissing him.

But he's the one who wants to know what's in this for

him while simultaneously telling me there isn't a relation-ship in this for me, so who's the unresponsive one now?

I chew and watch the cars drive past. Any one of them could point a gun out the window and shoot us on its way by.

For a brief, silent second, fear drops into my stomach as heavy as a cannonball.

Then it's gone.

Craig nods and says, "We could die right now."

See? He doesn't need me to talk. He really does get it.

"I guess."

He says, "Did you like what I said in class? I thought I captured your cynical attitude pretty well."

I shrug.

This macaroni and cheese is so weird. What's wrong with normal macaroni and cheese? I wish I had the other half of my sandwich back. It's inside Craig now.

I could kiss him and taste it.

I shouldn't think about stuff like that when I'm pissed at him.

He says, "Can I tell you something about September eleventh? It's something I figured out the other day, and I guess I thought you might have something interesting to say about it. Or, you know, whatever."

I squeeze my fingernails into my palms.

He says, "Yeah. So here's what I'm thinking. I heard so much about how New York really came together as a city after September eleventh. You know, you guys regenerated and rejuvenated and there was this new sense of . . . of humanity? I keep reading that, is that true? You experienced this new togetherness?"

There were a lot of candles and rallies.

I crumple my empty raisin box in my hand.

He says, "I don't think that ever happened in D.C. We never bonded over September eleventh. We swept up and pretended there was never a mess, y'know, and isn't that really depressing?"

I shrug.

"We never came together. It was almost like . . . like we didn't even talk about what happened, because we were so wrapped up in what happened in New York. The Pentagon seemed like such . . . small potatoes." He plays with his shoe. "So maybe this wouldn't be so scary if the wound weren't still raw from nine eleven. Because all this panic is actually like . . . residual? I guess. Like it's left over from something else entirely, and we're just redirecting it onto this."

"None of it really happened in D.C.," I say.

He looks at me. "What?"

I don't look at him. "You guys didn't come together after September eleventh because September eleventh wasn't yours."

Now it's Craig who isn't saying anything. I hazard a

glance, and he looks a lot like I probably did when he was talking, hands clenched, nostrils twitching. The difference is, I notice that he's upset and he didn't notice I was. The similarity is, neither one of us gives a shit.

"A hundred and eighty-nine people died," he says eventually. "A hundred and eighty-nine."

"Nearly *three thousand* in New York. The Pentagon *wasn't* the towers."

"You don't know what the fuck you're talking about, Lio."

"Comparing a hundred eighty-nine to twenty-seven hundred is *exactly* the same as comparing these shootings to nine eleven."

He makes his eyes smaller. "No, it isn't."

I raise an eyebrow.

"Because!" he says. "Because nine eleven happened! Because it felt like something! Because . . . it isn't all about the numbers. It's not . . . God, dead people isn't just *counting*. That isn't what I meant. That isn't what I was trying to say at all."

I pick at my jeans and shake my head.

It is.

How else do you measure this shit?

He takes his apple out of his lunch box and squeezes it. "The whole country cared about New York City. No one gave a shit about us. Half the newspapers outside of the US didn't even mention us, all they cared about was New

York. I went into the city afterward and it was like . . ."

The fact that he has to specify that he went into D.C. makes it all the more clear that he is a fucking Marylander, for God's sake. Soon the Virginians are going to be encroaching on our grief. Then what, Indiana? Fuck this shit.

I say, "The newspapers cared about us because we got *owned.* And Washington, D.C., was the only city in the entire fucking country who didn't give New York any bit of sympathy." My throat hurts. I don't want to do this shit anymore.

Craig throws his apple in the dirt. "We had our own problems!"

"You had a fucking inferiority complex."

He crosses his arms and now neither of us is looking at the other.

But he *doesn't* know. He wasn't there. What does he even know about dying? He's been so alive his whole life it makes me want to throw up.

And to talk about 9/11 as this inspiring experience, what the fuck is that? 9/11 was numbers and death and fire. It wasn't a city giving itself a group hug. I'm so sick of people trying to make it something pretty. It's just so Lifetime movie.

I stand up in time to see that Craig's crying.

It's not the first time I've seen him cry. The boy broke down during a History Channel segment on the War of 1812 in American Civ a few weeks ago, for God's sake.

It still makes me pause. I can't help it. I don't like crying.

I wish I knew what to say.

"You don't know what you're talking about," he says.

And suddenly words fall out of my mouth. "*I* don't know? What did nine eleven mean to you? What does it mean to anyone who didn't see the towers fall?"

His eyes are cat-narrowed, and he yells, "My boyfriend's fucking father didn't die in the fucking towers!"

I swallow.

Okay, so I didn't know that. I didn't know Cody's father died in the Pentagon. Craig should have told me that a long time ago.

I hate when people do this. I hate when people hide their cards to feel secret and strong. That's no way of dealing with anything. I don't pretend shit didn't happen to me. I don't stay up all night instead of going to therapy.

And he called Cody his boyfriend. Not ex-boyfriend. Just boyfriend.

So instead of apologizing, I swallow again and say, "A hundred and eighty-nine. It's not the same."

But Craig is crying hard now, and he won't look at me. I reach my hand out a little, but he doesn't move. I don't know what to do.

I pack his lunch up and leave it at his feet. I pack my lunch up, and I go.

Then I hit a freshman. I was getting so much better about that, too. I feel awful about it, so I turn myself in.

They don't suspend me, but they call my dad to pick me up. Because of the sniper, I'm not allowed to wait for him outside. Clearly they don't know where Craig and I eat.

And I realize, while I'm standing here with the principal by the front door, watching for my father, that I am worried about Craig. Out there, crying, unprotected.

Dad's pissed when he gets here. He had to leave work to pick me up. They should have let Jasper bring me home.

Dad walks me to the car in a zigzag pattern and says, "Well, I guess you'll have something to tell Adelle this afternoon, huh?"

Craig and his lunch are both gone.

Dad asks if I need ice for my hand, but I don't answer him. I really, really don't feel like talking. Adelle's going to have a great time with me today.

CRAIG

THINGS I ALWAYS LIKED ABOUT LIO:

The gaps between his canines and the rest of his teeth that make him look like a vampire or a really dangerous puppy.

His stupid multicolored hair that he never lets me see because of those hats he wears even though he isn't cold.

The fact that the teachers stopped making him take his hats off after the first week, probably because his hair is so fucked up.

The scar from the central line he had, and how he wears tank tops that let it show, and he doesn't care if people ask, he just says "cancer" and gives them a small smile to know he's not offended and he's not upset and he's not dead, and he plays with it, running his fingers across it and pinching the scar tissue when he's concentrating and he thinks no one's looking.

His voice, low and gravelly, like he's always getting over a cold.

Things I now hate:

His stupid smiles he makes me work for.

His stupid multicolored hair that he never lets me see because of those hats he wears even though he isn't cold.

The fact that I probably won't be mad at him in a few hours because he's so fucking shiny, he's like this star in my head and I can't get him out, and he's shining all bright and he's keeping me awake and I keep thinking about him but I don't think he's any more ready for me than I am for him, even though he probably thinks he is because he probably thinks he's all fixed up and shit, and he's not, and I'm not ready, I'm not, because I don't know how to be ready, but in a few hours I won't be mad at him anymore, and that sucks. I don't know what to do with that.

The tank tops that show off his arms.

Cancer boy cancer boy cancer boy cancer boy, I get it.

His silence.

So Cody's dad's death pretty much destroyed my boy, and as much as we didn't want it to destroy us, as hard as we worked, as hard as *I* worked . . .

God, I held on. I held on so hard, for months.

When he was screaming. When he was crying. When he was telling me he hated me and why hadn't I died instead. That time he slapped me across the face and shrieked "Bring him back bring him back *right now*." The time he shoved me across the room and told me if he ever saw me again he'd kill me himself, and called me two hours later, baby I'm so sorry, baby I'm just so sad and I don't know what to do and my therapist says I BLAH BLAH BLAH.

When he said he was going to buy a gun and get revenge himself, and I told him no—not because I thought that was wrong, but because I knew he wouldn't go to Afghanistan and I was worried he would go to school or his mother or his therapist. Or me.

So they eventually shipped him off, not to Afghanistan, but to some hospital and then some boarding school, and I never visited him, not once, and it took so long before he asked me to visit, and it should be simple to say no, I can't, I won't do it again, I can't, but it isn't, because he fell asleep crying in my arms so many times, and he called me Lollipop, and he told me I was the only thing, the only thing in the entire huge bad scary world, that helped.

So fuck frozen cold hearts, because who are they helping?

Fuck you, frozen cold heart.

× × ×

The school says those of us who don't drive can't stand outside waiting for a ride today, that we have to stay inside and stay safe. They have someone stationed outside with a walkie-talkie, and they call out our names when our parents get here. Except in my case it turns out to be not a parent, but a Todd.

I give him a hug because I'm the one who needs one, today.

"Were there any new—" I start to ask, and he shakes his head. It feels like a million years since someone's been shot. Maybe it's over. I say, "Can we stop for ice cream or something?"

"I . . . think we should go home, Craigy." Todd has this way of darting his eyes back and forth when he drives, like he thinks any minute someone's going to run out from behind some bushes and throw himself in front of our car. And he's doing it even more right now.

I say, "But I'm hungry, because I didn't even get to eat half my macaroni and cheese, and school was really boring. Criminally boring. Illegally boring. And I'm hungry."

"God, you're like two years old. Try a little perspective? There's a maniac out there."

I don't say, *there are like twenty million maniacs out there at any given moment, and none of them have ever shot me before.*

I turn away and look out the window. I guess I probably

don't usually see a lot of people standing outside their houses on my drive home from school, but everything still seems eerily empty.

There aren't any children trekking down the sidewalk with backpacks. That's what feels so wrong.

I say, "The kids aren't walking home from school."

"Not so surprising."

"That doesn't even make any sense at all. No one's shot any kids."

"And I think they want to keep it that way. The police chief said today, 'your children are safe in school.' If I were a parent . . ." Todd messes up his hair. "If I were a parent, I'd want to minimize the time spent between home and school as much as possible."

And just that minute, the announcer interrupts the international news to tell us there's been another shooting. It was pretty far away, this one—over an hour by Beltway, all the way in Virginia. Long-range rifle. They're "not sure" if it's the same shooter.

Todd curses softly. "Yeah, like it hasn't been enough time for him to get to Virginia."

"It could be a her. I don't think anyone's even considering it could be a her." I don't know. I think girls can do the shitty stuff guys do, now, because the first time Lio told me his mom left, I had the urge to tell him he misspoke. No, your dad left. Moms don't leave.

Fuck Lio.

Todd says, "I don't want you out looking for animals today."

I look up. "Todd, are you kidding?" Did Dad get him to say this? Did he think I wouldn't argue if it came from Todd? Arguing with Todd is my after-school activity. "So what am I supposed to do, avoid every single time that I could possibly be outside? I can't just wait until the sniper's all done to find my animals."

He shakes his head, watching the road. "It's not safe to be wandering around. Look, I know you think you're invincible, but—"

"Okay, look, can we be completely fucking honest? Doesn't everyone think they're invincible? I mean, you should know, isn't that why people kill themselves, because they're so convinced the world won't just boot them off on its own?"

He doesn't say anything.

"I mean," I say, "everyone's always talking about how it's a teenage thing, how we haven't developed the part of our brain that's counting down our seconds left to live or something, but I think it's got to be just part of being an individual and not being, I don't know, a thing or a city. Come on, big brother, educate me, tell me the truth. Isn't there something in you that says you're not going to die, not because you're special or privileged or *worthy* but just because you're *Todd*?"

Todd says, "Are you listening to anything I'm saying?

It's not *Todd* I'm worried about. You're staying in tonight. Get some homework done. Maybe even get some sleep, for God's sake. You look like shit."

Todd's protectiveness would mean more if I thought he really liked me and didn't just not want another dead body on his conscience.

I say, "Whoever this guy is, he's in Virginia right now. Even if he hightails it straight to our backyard, it'll be another hour at least. Can't I go look now?"

Todd exhales. "Fine."

"Thanks, big brother." I straddle the line between sarcastic and sincere. He chews on his lip. I hope I'm not mean to anyone else the way I'm mean to Todd.

I'm on the walkway to the metro station, and I'm thinking about how I still haven't seen anyone have sex here. Todd has all the luck.

I can see the pizza place and the Jewish supermarket from here, and I can see everyone in the parking lot running from the cars into the stores and back again.

"She's not here," I say out loud, "she's in Virginia." But I can't pretend watching them run doesn't shake me a little. It shakes me more than any of the news reports. I still don't think I have anything to be scared about, but it bothers me that they're scared. It bothers me in a way I can't shrug off.

I walk down to the grocery store like I can fix something,

and there on a lamppost is a poster saying that someone a few neighborhoods over found a three-legged dog. And suddenly nothing else in the whole world is important in any way.

Casablanca.

I memorize the phone number on the poster and recite it to myself again and again while I'm running home. I run faster than anyone in that entire parking lot.

Only eight to go.

One dog.

Three cats.

Three rabbits.

A guinea pig.

The news replays the police chief telling us we're safe at school while we eat dinner. Casablanca has his head on my knee.

My mom takes my hand. "If you want to talk," she says, "know that your father and I are available, okay? For anything you need to get off your chest."

"That's really nice, really, but I don't want to talk. This doesn't have anything to do with me. See, I'm just worried about Michelangelo and Beaumont and Hail and Marigold and Shamrock and Peggy and Zebra and Carolina." I still want to believe that Mom's been out helping the families of the victims, but that's not really the type of social work she does.

Mom gives me a gentle smile. "I talked to the woman at the shelter today and gave her your descriptions." She has to specify mine because last time she gave her own descriptions and I told her but how are they going to know that Shamrock's tail leans to the left when he's happy, or that Zebra will only eat if all his food is level, or that Beaumont has a meow like a fire alarm, and what if those are the keys to identifying them?

"Good," I say.

Dad has his own problems, like the stack of papers he brought to the dinner table, and he rubs his face to show us how very busy he is. He's flipping through the papers between mouthfuls of baked salmon. Parents are harassing him like he's a suspect in the shootings: "Why can't my child go outside for recess? This is ridiculous." "What took you so long to cancel outdoor recess? Do you know how many children you put at risk?"

I need to get away from all of this. I put Casablanca and Kremlin on their leashes, and I nudge lazy Jupiter with the toe of my shoe. "Time for a walk," I tell them.

"Not tonight," Dad says. "Just tie them up out back, all right?"

"They hate that."

"Craig," he says, in that tone that's like, *I'm one step away from middle-naming you.*

I breathe in and then out, really slowly. "Okay." I tie them up out back while my parents watch to make sure I'm not outside for too long. I sit by the door and press my hand against the glass so the dogs can see me, so maybe they'll feel like I'm with them. They bark and spin in circles on their rope, and if anyone shoots them, I have this feeling I'll kill my dad.

Cody—

I still haven't heard from you and I'm worried, wondering if you're okay and everything. Is school getting busy? Is this when you take the SATs or something?

I forgot to tell you, when I saw your mom she showed me some of the paintings you mailed her. They were beautiful. I loved the one of me, I really did, but she wouldn't let me keep it. Maybe let her know if she can send it to me?

Miss you,

Love, C

It's seven o'clock. In the evening. I need to sleep, I need to stop thinking. I need to sleep.

The real question isn't who broke into the house, at least not for me, because I don't care, because it happened and it's over and I'm getting the animals back and everything's going to be fine.

But why did the animals leave? Just because the doors were open? Just because they had an excuse to?

My parents always thought I was so stupid and I thought I was so lucky keeping my guinea pig and my cats and my dogs and my bird together and no one ever had to be in a cage and no one was ever locked up and no one ever hurt anybody. It was like a little miracle, and then someone broke through our doors and left everything open and they all ran away together, and that's why I don't have any animals. The breaking-in, the breaking the windows, the breaking apart, the violence, none of that had anything to do with it. They only left because the door was open. Just freedom had to do with it, or maybe fear, and that's all that mattered in the end, and I fall asleep sitting up and wake up a minute later, and these are the times when I don't believe that all the animals are ever going to be not gone.

"Weren't you happy here?" I whisper.

I tried. I tried so hard.

I'm still trying. I'm grasping grasping grasping at no reward.

The woman they shot today, when I was on the way home from school? She didn't die. It's another reason not to be scared. There's always the chance you won't get shot, and there's always the chance you'll get shot and you won't die. There are so many ways to survive. Why does everyone act like we're hopeless?

LIO

I'M MAKING ANOTHER PLAY-DOH SNOWMAN.

I wish I could go for a jog instead.

Adelle says, "Would you like to talk about what's going on this week?"

I shrug.

"Lio."

I say, "If you mean what's going on in my life."

"You don't want to talk about the sniper?"

I shake my head.

My dad came inside my therapist's building with me, his arms around me like a coat. We ran. He's not supposed to come inside here. This is meant to be my place. That was a rule my last therapist made, and Dad and I both agreed it worked well. I need a place.

And then he came in here and said, "Adelle, right?" and shook her hand. And damn it, I had to pee, so they had a whole minute and fifteen seconds alone together. Dad probably told her I wet the bed until I was eight (give me a break, I had other things on my mind), and Adelle probably told him about my snowman-molding fetish. Fuck everything.

"Okay," Adelle says. "So what's going on in your life this week?"

I think of better things. Things that aren't honestly part of my life, and ways that I wish I were.

I shrug. "I'm in love."

And I screwed up so badly, but I'm not going to mention that part right now.

Adelle's writing something down. This must be the kind of moment therapists live for. I'm a success story. Isn't it thanks to years of therapists that I *can* fall in love?

Adelle smiles. "With Craig?"

"Who else? Of course Craig."

She laughs a little. "You're talkative today."

I frown.

"Oh, I'm sorry. I didn't say that to shut you up."

I shrug.

She sighs. "Damn."

Small smile.

She closes her notebook. "Well? What's he like?"

"Tall."

"Yeah?"

"Like nearly six feet."

"That's not that tall." Then she looks at me and bites her cheek. "All right, that's tall for you, fair enough. Keep going."

I look out the window. There's a nice red car parked on the sidewalk. Are people worried their cars are going to get shot? If you have a car like that, you probably spend more time on it than you do on yourself. Why am I thinking about this?

I'm wondering what kind of car Cody's dad drove. That's not right.

Cody's dad.

I didn't know him. But Craig did. He actually knows someone who died on 9/11. And I don't know why the fact that Craig knew someone who died in the Pentagon is making what happened here seem like a bigger deal. I already knew how many people died. This isn't new information.

I'm not Craig; I always knew that everyone was equally vulnerable. That one person isn't a more shocking loss than another.

That's why you have to count them one by one. That's what makes more people dying worse. It's just math.

And it's the reason little things—one person dying, six people dying—are things to get over. You go to therapy if you have to, and you learn how to tuck them away.

I'm still wondering about Cody's father's car.

Craig doesn't have a car. I don't have a car. I'm clinging to these thoughts like they mean something.

Adelle says, "Lio. You okay?"

This is ridiculous. Craig is fine. Almost every single person in this city is fine.

I swallow. "He has a thing with animals."

She raises her eyebrows. "A thing?" She totally thinks I mean something kinky.

I breathe well enough to smile.

"He keeps them," I say.

"He's your first boyfriend, right?"

"Yeah. He's not my boyfriend."

"Are you his first?"

"No." I pick at the couch. "He had a boyfriend who went crazy. Now he's alone. And the animals are gone. Now he's really alone."

But safe.

"What about his family?" Adelle says.

I pick at the couch. "He has one of those fantasy nuclear families. They could be on a sitcom."

"How does that make you feel about your family?"

I look at her. "We were talking about Craig."

"Craig isn't my patient. I was using him as a method to get you talking. How do you feel about your family, when you compare it to his?"

I'm not sure she's supposed to reveal her secret therapist ways to me. Though I do know a lot about therapy, now. I've memorized whole sections of the Diagnostic Statistical Manual, after years of sitting in waiting rooms. I could start my own business. I'd be like Lucy in *Peanuts*.

I keep thinking about Charlie Brown, because I don't want to babble about my family. That's not going to help me. It's just going to make me angry again. And if I'm angry again, I'm going to shut down and waste my time here. I want to talk about Craig. I squish my snowman.

"All right," Adelle says. "So you hit a kid at school today."

This is why my dad shouldn't be allowed to come in. Two minutes and he gives things away.

"Yeah." I'm biting the inside of my lower lip.

"I know you had aggression problems at your old school."

I nod. It's not like I ever really hurt anyone. I always messed with kids who were bigger than me. They never hit me back. Everyone thought I was brave. I don't know anymore.

"Why did you do it today?" she says.

"I was . . . angry. I had this fight with Craig. It wasn't a big deal." I breathe out and say, "Why am I still so angry?"

She leans toward me. "About Craig?"

"We're not talking about Craig. About my mom, I guess."

"Abandonment is a scary feeling. It makes sense you're still angry about her leaving. People take years to recover from divorce. That's still significant trauma, even if you have other shit you'd rather be worrying about." Even though she's Adelle of "a little fucked up" fame, it still throws me when she curses. I think she does it to be cool.

"That one makes sense. But about my brother. About cancer." I cross my arms. "I've read pretty much everything about twin death. I realize I'm allowed to be messed up about it for the rest of my life. If that's what I want." I'm allowed to make a full-scale tragedy out of my dead brother. Sometimes I hate the things I am allowed to do.

Adelle says, "Yes."

"And . . ." I'm losing this.

But she says, "You're doing really well, Lio."

I get the words out as fast as I can. "And I've accepted that it's always going to be a hard thing for me. It's never going to be like I was born a single." God, my mouth is sore. I hate talking. Fuck everything. "I'm okay with struggling with this. I really am. I've accepted that."

Adelle nods.

"This can be a part of my life."

"That sounds very healthy," she says, like she isn't sure.

I say, "But shouldn't I be past the part where I'm *so* angry?"

Adelle says, "Lio, you have to understand that grief doesn't work in neat little stages. Bargaining, depression, and yes, anger, they're part of grief, but they don't come conveniently in order, waiting their turn. Does that make sense? It's all right that you're angry. You're fifteen. You don't need a reason to be angry."

I exhale. "I'm done talking. Can you talk for a while?"

"You don't pay me to lecture you."

"My dad pays you." I'm so tired. Sometimes I use cancer as an excuse when I get so exhausted even though I sleep and exercise and eat well. I tell people it still affects me. That's total bullshit. I'm healthy.

My last therapist said I was tired because I was depressed. I don't think that's what it is. One of my friends from New York has depression, and it eats him alive. I'm not depressed. I'm . . . fucked up.

She says, "You are allowed to feel guilty for surviving."

"Everyone tells me not to."

"People are afraid to acknowledge that there's validity in that. You did live. Your brother did not. That *is* something to feel conflicted about."

"I don't wish I were dead or anything."

"What do you wish?"

"That Theo would be back. And fifteen. But that's stupid."

"It isn't."

I pull at my jeans. They're black, and they're dirty. "I wish I could come in here just to talk about being in love. Like you were my friend or something, I don't know."

CRAIG

I NEED TO SLEEP. I NEED TO STOP THINKING AND I
need to stop thinking about how I need to sleep.

It's four. In the morning. I need to sleep.

This is when my thoughts start to get so very very weird,
when everything is on an axis and tilting, and this is how
many hours of sleep you really need to miss. This is how many
emails from Cody you need to not get. Here I am.

Sandwich sits on my feet and curls up and snores.

"Sandwich," I tell her. "Do you get sick of being alone?"

She so doesn't care at all. It's like nobody in this whole
world gives a shit, least of all Lio, least of all me.

✗ ✗ ✗

And it's not like it's easy to sleep or even possible to run out of things to think about for even a second because, ta-da, here's this email I got a few hours ago.

Craigy—

Sorry this took me so long.

I'm sorry about your friend's dad, and it took me a while to figure out that maybe that was all I can say—I'm sorry. For being a jerk about it. I didn't know. And it sucks.

Truth is I talk a big game about September 11th, but I didn't know anyone who died. It feels special because it's home.

Truth is, I really, really miss New York.

I'm freaked out tonight. I keep hearing things in the apartment upstairs.

See you tomorrow. No. Shit. It's Friday. See you on Monday. Damn it.

Lio

God, so what do I do with this? I've been staring at it for the past million and a half hours.

Why is the only thought in my head, *you can't fool me, you were born on Long Island?*

I am looking for excuses to be angry. I am picking apart the sentences for bits that could be offensive and I am wondering if I am too young to have issues with intimacy.

I hear Todd making breakfast. Speaking of talking a big game, when does he sleep? It must be while I'm at school, but it's kind of crazy to think that my family exists when I'm not here.

I go upstairs.

He's throwing scoops of coffee into the coffeemaker. "Good morning," he tells me.

"Yeah." I slump at the table and bury my head in my arms.

I hear him pause in his scooping. "You okay?"

"Yeah. You?"

He exhales. "A kid killed himself on the phone with me tonight. I was talking him down, doing everything you're supposed to do, and I hear the gunshot. And I keep saying his name—Taylor, Taylor—like, praying it went off in his hand . . ."

"Christ."

"And it's like . . . of all the things to hear right now. A gunshot." He shakes his head.

I don't know how he can think of the sniper when he

just heard someone die, someone, an actual person, die, and how he can think that the shot he heard is reminiscent of the sniper, and not the other way around.

"How old was he?" I ask.

"Fifteen, sixteen." He turns the coffeemaker on and starts fixing oatmeal. I feel like he'll keep making something new as soon as he finishes what he's cooking, and he'll never sit down and eat, and that's my brother, really. He says, "I'm sorry about Dad, at dinner."

"It's fine."

"He's not very sensitive of you, and I'm sorry. He just doesn't understand you, you know?"

"I think I'm the one who's supposed to talk about how misunderstood I am, and you're supposed to come back at me with lots of elderly wisdom or something. Can I have a glass of milk?"

"May I." He actually says that, and then he pours a glass for me. He overfills the glass, and milk spills onto the counter.

"Don't cry," I say, and he snickers a little. I wipe it up with a paper towel.

"Thanks," he says.

"It's my milk." I take the glass. "Besides, the cats would be up here in a second if I hadn't jumped on it."

He says, "That's where Dad's issues come from. It's not just the fact that he doesn't know how to deal with anyone but elementary schoolers—though let's not pretend that's not an issue. He has no idea why you got all the animals and what to do with the fact that you essentially took over this house last year. Or let them take over the house, at least."

"I don't know what to say. I love them."

"God, I know, Craig."

"And it's not like it matters because now they're gone." And I start shaking, and then here is Todd hugging me, and here I am crying again because I am apparently four, or however old he told me I was.

"Hey," he says. "It's okay. We're going to find them."

"Flamingo already died."

"Who?"

"The bird." I breathe hard. "Dead bird. Now what? How many other dead animals are out there? And Dad won't let me go look for them . . ."

"Come on," he says. He lets go of me and puts on his coat.

"What?"

"It's not as if you have school to get ready for, yeah? And I don't need sleep. I have Saturday nights off. Come on, let's go look."

When we're looking around, calling and whistling and swinging our flashlights, Todd tells me about this girlfriend he had who used to leave letters in his locker folded up like frogs or swans. I don't know why he thinks this story will make me feel better, but it does.

He doesn't have a girlfriend now. He says he's too busy.

"Is that how it works?" I say. "Is having a girlfriend or a boyfriend something like a job, like you need room in your schedule?"

"Well, no, Craig, but they call it a commitment for a reason. You don't need to block out time in your day for a relationship, but you do need to have time to nurture it. Time to give a shit about someone else. And sometimes you don't have room for another person."

So I guess we have a capacity for things we can care about and then we reach it, and we're screwed. That sounds like I'm judging Todd, but I'm not. I think that it's a shame that he loves a few people so incredibly much that he's used up all his love and he can't spread it around, and that those people are me and Mom and Dad and people who call him on the brink of death who he loves with every bit of him for those five minutes, and the problem is that none of us give that much of a shit about him, because we don't know how. Because I see him looking at me and caring so much and trying to connect to me and failing failing failing, and I don't know how to help him, because I don't know what I need from him. I don't know what I need from anyone.

I'm so worried about him. And God, what if something happens to one of us? It would be like losing all your money in the stock market. That's a horrible analogy, but it's what

I mean. It's just that I think there are some good reasons to keep a foot on the ground. That's all I'm saying.

Todd says, "And you've been in a relationship more recently than I have. You know how it is."

"Not really," I say, because I never had trouble making room for Cody. But Todd looks at me funny, so I say, "Yeah. I don't know. It's been a really long time. Sometimes I think I'm remembering it wrong. Like it wasn't . . . how I thought it was." I'll decide that I'm pretending everything was so much easier and better and sweeter than it possibly could have been, in reality. Was he really that gorgeous? Were we really that molded together? And then I see a picture or I hear a song I heard with him and, yes, it was just as incredible, and he's just as gone.

Todd puts his hand on my shoulder. "I'm sorry. We don't have to talk about this." He lowers his voice. "Though you brought it up."

"Well, yeah. I'm thinking about it."

"Look," I say.

Todd shifts a little so he's in front of me. "What?"

I aim my flashlight at a bush. "There's something moving."

He says, "Let me handle it."

"It's not going to shoot me." I approach on my hands and knees and make kissing noises. "Hey, baby baby, come out?"

He mews a little and comes out. Holy shit, it's Shamrock. He's as cute as I remembered.

"Todd, it's Shamrock!"

He breathes out. "I'm so glad we found one."

And, for a minute, Shamrock is my whole world. It's like when I adopt them for the first time, and for a second all I have to do is keep a little animal clean and fed and warm and that is enough, and this kitten needs nothing else from me but love and there is nothing my love won't fix for him. I can hold him against my chest and tell him I love him and there you go, he's purring. That's all he needs. His fur is so soft. "Thank you, Todd," I say.

One dog.

Two cats.

Three rabbits.

A guinea pig.

I have this weekend friend. He's only my friend on the weekends, because we don't go to the same school and we don't care enough to track each other down. But on Saturdays we have karate together, so after that we usually get Slurpees or something. His name is Mansfield, which is one of the most unfortunate things I've ever experienced.

He's not very good at karate, either. I don't know why he's in my class, but there are only six other kids in the class with us, so maybe they'd feel too bad about dumping him. Anyway, it's not like I'm great at karate. We're probably the failure class and no one cared to tell us, but I still like doing it. It keeps me from being an angry young man, I guess.

After class we pack up our shit and I ask him if he wants to walk to the 7-Eleven, and he says, "I don't know, Craig. I don't know if this is the perfect week to be walking around looking for a Slurpee, you know?"

What the fuck?

I say, "Come on, it's like half a block."

"It's right by a gas station."

"Yeah . . . ?"

Mansfield looks at me. "Come on, Craig, don't play dumb. That's where everyone's getting shot: gas stations and parking lots. I don't want to die before I have sex."

"So I'm home free, then." I give him this big smile, and Mansfield looks at me with this face, and it's so worth him thinking I'm straight if it makes him this jealous of me. Heh. I mean, he could always be jealous of the fact that I've slept with a boy, too, or also that I own him at karate, or that I'm not too afraid to get a Slurpee, but this is easier.

So I think, whatever, I'll go get a Slurpee myself, it's not as if I really value Mansfield's company. But when I walk out of the karate studio, there's my mom, station wagon idling in front of the place, and she says, "Craig, come on, hurry into the car." Jesus Christ. It makes me want to wear fluorescent pink clothing and jump up and down. I need to send Lio to her, to tell her exactly what my chances are of getting shot. Next to nothing. Next to *nothing*. This is all so stupid.

LIO

I DON'T THINK THERAPY ON FRIDAY HELPED ME. I probably should have sucked it up and talked about the sniper. Maybe that's what I needed. Maybe that would fix me.

My dad is on the phone with one of my faraway sisters. Jasper and Michelle are at the mall buying Chrismakkuh presents. They asked me if I wanted to come. I don't know why I said no. I like the mall. I never buy anything, but I like to walk around and look at people.

My therapist has been on me about that, lately, how I always say no to things I would like. I don't think I've ever had a drink on an airplane because I always say, "No thank you, I'm fine," too quickly to consider something. It's ridiculous that these are the problems that my dad pays so much for me to talk about.

My real problem is that Craig hasn't answered my email.

I should probably do some homework, but I have a hard time convincing myself that homework really matters. I haven't done any reading for a class since middle school, but I still get As on all my papers.

It's depressing that those As are, so far, the entirety of my success story. When I was nine, I thought I would drop out of school and join a band and travel all over the world. And now here I am, and whether I do my homework or not, graduation has started to look inevitable. I got out of dying from cancer, but I can't get out of graduating from high school.

Maybe I'm destined for a middle American life. That's probably why my twin got killed off. Your average desk bitch doesn't have an identical twin.

This doesn't explain why I'm gay. This doesn't explain *anything*. God, I need to shut up. Or maybe say some of this stupid shit out loud so it will go away.

I sit up.

I should probably tell my therapist this, except she's not supposed to listen to me say this bullshit stuff. She's paid to weigh in on my bullshit stuff. I don't need perspective on this. I don't need to be told that all of this comes down to twin guilt.

I had one therapist who was convinced all my problems came from feeling my brother even though he isn't here. Phantom pain. Like losing a limb.

I gave that some thought and came to the reluctant conclusion that it was definitely bullshit. I don't feel Theodore. I don't remember how eight years old felt. Most of the time I'm grateful for that.

There's this bird outside my window. It's so loud. I wish someone would shoot it. Ha.

So this is dumb, but every Saturday I end up considering calling Mom. I hate talking on the phone, and I'd probably end up just breathing loudly like a creeper. I don't know her number, either. I'd have to ask Dad. That would be horrible. So I never call, but I always think about it.

I'm thinking about it right now when my cell phone rings. Who the fuck would call me? I check the screen, but it's not Craig.

Fuck Alexander Graham Bell. I hate being forced to talk.

"Hello?"

"Hey, Lio, this is Amelia."

Amelia. It could be worse, easily. She's from school. She's definitely into me. She's also really good at statistics and has a knack for witty IMs, so I keep her. But if she thinks our relationship has progressed to phone calls, I feel bad for leading her on.

I say, "Hey."

She says, "So sorry for cold-calling, and ohmyGod this is so lame but my dad realized our country club—I know, I totally wouldn't blame you if you hung up now—closes like tomorrow or the next day and we still have all these kind of pseudo-free dinners still available under our membership. If we don't use them, the money kind of goes to waste."

She leaves a space here for me to say something.

"So, anyway," she continues. "My parents can't go tonight, so they told me, 'Amelia, why don't you invite someone from school,' so I was wondering if you'd like to go with me?"

I say, "Oh."

There are a lot of reasons I should say no to her. The fact that I'm gay is probably the first reason, but it's not the only one by any stretch. There's the fact that I'm in love with someone else, unavailable though he may be. Or that making small talk over small portions isn't exactly my thing.

So, I should say no, but apparently my *no thanks I'm fine* disease doesn't apply here. I say, "Let me ask my dad, okay?"

That is the worst thing I've ever said. I essentially just cut off my penis.

I say, "We might have plans. I can get out of them." I realize I'm trying to compensate for what I said about asking Dad for permission. I'm trying to get her to think I might be cool. *Way to go. Woo back the straight girl.* Jesus, I can't win.

"Oh, sure," she says. "Just call me back?"

"Yeah. Um, I'll IM you." I hang up because I sound like a jackass and that shit needs to end.

Okay, Dad is going to tell me what to do. Even though I haven't come out to my family, I'm pretty sure there's an unspoken understanding that I'm gay ever since I sang "Man, I Feel Like a Woman" in my mother's high heels, completely bald, for one of our family talent shows.

I don't remember this, but the pictures are pretty fabulous.

I step into the kitchen. "Dad?"

"He's napping," Jasper says. Shit, when did they get home? The shoes Michelle's wearing must be new, because she's studying the reflection of her feet on the oven.

"I don't know that they're exactly right," she says, and then she looks up at me. "What's up? You look like shit."

Wow thanks. "I just . . . I have something I need to ask him, okay?"

"Okay," Michelle says. "God. You don't have to verbally abuse us."

Jasper says, "Leave him alone. Can I help, Li?" She gives me a hug. "Is everything okay?"

Maybe I really do look like shit. I say, "This girl invited me to dinner. I don't know what to say."

My sisters light up like candles. "Oh, my God. Oh, my God!" Jasper spins me. "Oh, my God, Lio, your first date! This is bigger than your bar mitzvah!"

I hope someone gives me money and cufflinks for this.

"What are you going to wear?" Michelle asks me. "Please tell me you are *not* going to wear a T-shirt. Let's not wear anything with words on it, Lio, okay?" She's touching me all over like she's trying to clean me off. "And something besides black? You must have colors in your closet somewhere. You have some red and pink, don't you? If we choose one to accent the black . . ."

Oh, God. They think I'm straight.

I say, "I haven't said yes yet . . ."

Jasper says, "Oh, Jesus, Lio, don't play hard to get. Call her and tell her you're coming. You don't have to act so uptight just because you're gay."

Now I'm entirely confused.

"Go get ready!" Jasper says. "Call her! Get dressed! Just don't kiss her at the end, that would be cruel. Unless you like her! Don't limit yourself, Lio!"

"Remember, wear *nothing* with words!" Michelle calls after me. "And find a hat that isn't falling apart. Don't you dare show her your hair!"

I do not understand my life.

Dad drives me. Maybe my sisters are aware this is all some kind of ruse, but I'm getting the feeling my father has no idea this date isn't going to end in marriage and children. He's babbling on about his first date, and his first car he drove to go pick her up. And how in his day they didn't have these fancy electric car window openers, you had to crank them down by hand. God, I want to crank my head off right now.

He says, "You brought money to pay?"

"It's her country club, Dad. She's going to pay. Or her parents."

"Oh, then they might give you a menu without prices. I'm not sure. It's been a long time since I ate at a country club. But don't order anything too expensive. But don't order anything too cheap, either, that'll insult her. It's best to stick with some kind of chicken or fish."

I like how he thinks I'm straight but has managed to deduce that I'm basically the girl in this situation.

"And don't linger outside," he says. "You know."

I say, "Yeah, I know."

He doesn't need to tell me.

My heart starts pounding like after a nightmare, so I close my eyes and take some deep breaths. I know how to calm myself down. I just hate that, ever since that argument with Craig, I've had to do it so often.

There is no reason for me to be scared. No one has been shot in hours. Feeling vulnerable isn't new to me.

Thinking my vulnerability is significant is.

The voice in my head saying, *Cody's dad shouldn't have died*—yeah, that is, too.

I don't know what's wrong with me, but this isn't the headspace I need to be in right now.

The outside of the country club is deserted. It's hard to walk in these stupid shoes. They're my dad's and too big. It's like my feet are fish. It takes me too long to get from the car to inside. I breathe.

Amelia is wearing a pink silky dress that falls off her shoulders. I realize now how poorly I know her. I don't think I would have recognized her if she weren't the only teenage girl standing alone. But she's funny over IM. And her dress is pretty.

She gives me a little wave. "Thanks so much for coming," she says. "I think if I hadn't found someone to treat, my dad would have been really concerned that I had no friends or something."

I smile a little. Is she familiar with the fact that I don't talk? I can't remember if she's ever tried to interact with me in real life. Why did she invite me? Maybe she really doesn't have any friends. At least that's something we have in common. That can be our conversation starter. Too bad I'm the official conversation finisher.

We get a table. There's a little useless candle between us. When I was a kid, my sisters and I used to set the napkins on fire whenever we were at a place nice enough to have candles at the tables. That wasn't very often, since every time we went, my sisters and I would try to set everything on fire.

Amelia makes small talk about movies. I nod and say a few words when I can. We order, and I get chicken in some kind of wine sauce. It's in the price range my dad would like, but it feels really gay. I feel like Amelia can tell, even though of course she doesn't say anything.

Really, I ordered it because it has the shortest name on the menu. Seriously, I'm pathological.

"So how are you liking D.C.?" she asks.

People around here have a weird habit of calling it D.C. This is Maryland.

I say, "It's okay."

The food tastes like something an old person would eat, but it's not so bad, really, just suspiciously easy to chew. I get self-conscious about how many sips I take from my water glass and how many times I have to wipe my mouth on the scratchy napkin. We're not talking anymore, and for the first time ever, I hate it. I hate the silence and I hate this date. Why did I let my sisters force me into this?

It's not like they pushed very hard. I folded.

I was afraid of saying no to something I would like. And look where that got me. I think I need to figure out what it is, exactly, I would like.

Besides a boy who won't have me.

I make a lot of efforts to smile at Amelia.

The evening's ending. Our plates are empty enough to not be embarrassing. She says she doesn't want dessert, and I don't drink coffee, so I guess that's it. She sees me checking my watch. "Is your dad going to pick you up?"

"Yeah. I'll call him. You?"

"Oh, I live just a little bit away, through the woods. I'm going to walk."

I look up quickly. "You're going to walk through the woods?"

"Yeah." She must catch my expression. She laughs a little, back in her throat. She sounds old. Old enough for the food. "Oh, don't look at me like that, Lio. Don't get paranoid like . . . I'll be fine."

I say, "Listen, my dad can drop you off."

"No, really. I brought shoes to walk in and everything. It'll help me burn off some of this dinner." She laughs. But she didn't eat that much, not enough to die for.

I say, "Hey . . . please?"

She blows me off again, and I don't know any other ways to ask.

Dad calls me when he's at the door. I run to the car.

"Did you have fun?" he asks me.

I nod and look out the window. Amelia's in the woods, alone.

She is probably, probably, probably not going to get shot.

Unless she gets shot, I don't think I'll remember her in a few years. But if she gets shot, I'll remember. I'll regret it forever. I'll get fucked up again.

Breathe.

Statistics. It is statistically impossible that she will die.

This is how I calm myself down.

Breathe.

Theo was a fluke.

Cody's dad shouldn't have died.

What do two flukes make?

"Dad?" I say.

He glances at me while he drives. His eyebrows are all together.

I say, "Are you scared?"

He nods. "Yeah."

"Okay." I look out the window again.

He doesn't ask me if I'm scared. I hope that's because he knows, not because he thinks I already have a therapist and he doesn't need to know.

He reaches underneath my cap and messes up my hair. I haven't had a cigarette in days, and it's really getting to me. But I'm too scared to step outside and smoke one. If my dad knew I smoked, he'd eat me alive. He'd cry.

CRAIG

I SLEEP.

I sleep.

Heavy, breathless, unbelievable, I sleep.

I sleep.

That was a horrible dream.

I look at my clock: 3:27 a.m. As soon as I swing my feet onto the floor, cold floor cold feet cold Craig, Kremlin starts pawing at my leg. No time like the present, so I hook the dogs up to their leashes and disable our new fancy burglar alarm. I make sure the cats don't get out, and we go for a run.

x x x

I wish I were a good runner.

In my dream, Cody was screaming at me to run faster, and I don't know what the metaphorical significance of this is because nothing about running ever happened to us. I could make it into some extended thing about me running into the Pentagon, but that feels like a stretch. A huge stretch, like a full stretch further than a regular stretch, even.

I don't think he and his father were that close. They never seemed to be. Once I saw them scream at each other so hard Cody's throat went raw, and that was when I was there, when company was there, and even though I didn't like to think of myself as company in my boyfriend's house, his mom kept going, "Quiet, *quiet,* we have company!" but they didn't listen. God knows what they did when I wasn't there. One time Cody showed up with a big bruise across his mouth and asked if he could sleep over, but that and the time he hit me are the only evidence I have, and even evidence isn't proof.

For a while after September 11th, it looked like he was going to be okay. Once they gave up hope that Mr. Carter was coming home—and that took a long time—he and his mom squished together and supported each other. Cody came over to my house all the time, and that was nice, to see him, to have a chance to make things right. He was sad.

We'd bake cookies. We'd have sex. We'd watch stupid movies, we'd cry, we'd fall asleep. We slept, in my bed upstairs, in my room upstairs.

Then around January he started to forget where he'd put things, kind of like Dad does, except Cody never had a head injury. And then he was returning phone calls I never made, and then he stopped sleeping. Stopped sleeping completely, and that was the beginning of the end, I guess. He lost his mind and maybe it's never coming back. At least, it's probably never coming back to me.

He hasn't emailed.

Why am I such a slow runner?

If I continue not to sleep, maybe I'll totally lose it and get shipped out to where he is. And I'll see what he's seen, and it'll be like I'm being him, like I understand. And someone will finally, finally, bring me to him. I'm so lame. Someone has to bring me to him? I'm not a damsel in distress. I could go. I could hop on a bus or go with his mom next time she invites me or I could beg Mom and somehow I could go.

I'm not going to go, but maybe I'll go insane.

My neighborhood is eerie and dark, but it's familiar, and I'm only circling it over and over. And, to be honest, more people have their lights on than I would have expected at this time of night. It's like they set out beacons for me.

The dogs are faster than I am. I'll never understand how

dogs can be so fast. These dogs could outrun me forever. I should have tied them up out back. They're going to get me so tired and I'll pass out and die, and then what?

Then what?

I stop in front of a house I don't know and pant with my hands on my knees. I feel my shoulder blades pressing against my sweater every time I breathe in. Maybe they'll turn into wings and I can fly away. Then I'd beat the dogs.

It's not that I really want to beat the dogs, it'd just be nice to know that I could.

I hear a soft growl, and I look to make sure the dogs are okay, but it's a car, old and slow, trembling its way across the block.

Its lights are off.

It comes toward me. It has tinted windows and I can't see the driver.

I straighten up.

It drives past me, wheels clanking. I can hear the torn-up tar on the sides of the sidewalk crunching under the tires. It gives me a half second of a heart attack, and then it's gone. That's what it left me with, a fucking half-second heart attack and then my heartbeat back and loud and clear, going *you're stupid you're stupid you're stupid.*

I stay out to see the sunrise, and when I get home . . . oh shit. My parents, both of them in their flannel pajamas, the ones I guess they wear when they're not going to have sex. I wish they'd had sex. That's really gross, but maybe they wouldn't be glaring at me if they had.

But they probably would be. I think adults can probably have sex and a life at the same time, which is sort of a foreign concept for me.

"Where the hell were you?" my dad says.

I hold up the dog leashes.

My father says, "Jesus, Craig. Can you really be this incredibly oblivious?"

"I'm not oblivious. I'm also not going to let my dogs, like, atrophy because a few people have been shot."

"A few *innocent people!*" my father says. "A few people who were shot for absolutely no reason except for *where they happened to be.*"

But . . . but, no, I'm calling bullshit, because entire lives are determined by where we happen to be. It's the only reason we care about the cities we care about. God, it's the only reason we fall in love. It's where you happen to be. I'm not going to spend my whole life fucking freaking out about it.

"I'm not going to get shot," I say. "You're not actually sitting here thinking that I'm going to get shot, come on."

Mom has her head in her hands. She says, "I know you're not. But you scared your father and me to death."

"But what are you scared of, if you know I'm not going to get shot?"

127

Mom breathes out. "I know it must seem to you like there are *so* many other people out there who could be—"

God, Lio and my mom and everyone need to shut up about numbers, I don't care, I don't care, I just care that I'm not going to die because I'm *not*.

I don't think I'm ever going to believe that I'm vulnerable the way other people are vulnerable, and fine, that's stupid. I get it. But all this shit keeps happening and I'm still here, so what else am I supposed to even think? I shut the door to the basement and tramp down the stairs. Fine. It's stupid. But I don't know how to change it. I don't know how to convince myself that I could be like the people I see on the news or the people I imagine at Cody's school. Do I need to put a gun to my own head to feel it? I'm not going to die, and this is my life, and I feel it in my fucking bones, so am I supposed to understand how it's possible to not be alive? Being alive is all that I am.

This is all such bullshit. Hiding. Running in zigzags. The only thing I have to do is be me. That's the way to not get shot. Be self-aware. I don't mean that the dead people didn't have a sense of identity or something. I just mean . . .

I don't know.

They weren't me.

I'm not going to die.

And I know how stupid it sounds, but even when I try to convince myself that it's the dumbest way ever to think,

I can't talk myself out of it. It's the same voice that keeps me from killing myself every time I want to a little. *If I'm dead, who's going to be me?*

My cousins were supposed to visit this Sunday from Pennsylvania, but now they're not because their parents don't think it's safe to be in Maryland. They're worried about the kids, and it's so stupid, because no one's been shot since Friday, and he lived, and there haven't been any kids.

"Your kids are safe at school." The police chief said so himself. I mean, if anyone knows, it's him. They're probably safer here than in Pittsburgh, if you take air pollution into account, and the fact that if you trip in Pittsburgh you'll probably get, like, speared through by a fucking piece of steel or some shit like that.

No emails from anybody, except that old one from Lio still sitting in my inbox. I'll answer it later, I will, I will I will I will. That movie we wanted to see, *Phone Booth?* They're postponing the release because they think it'll be too upsetting this close to the shootings. I bet Lio's really pissed off and confused about that, because even I can't believe the rest of the country even knows about the shootings, since I bet the same number of people have died in every single state in the United States this week, probably more, so God knows why they're postponing a movie because of us. I really am starting to sound like Lio, I think, and I wonder if that means I'm starting to think like him too. I'm wondering what it's like in Lio's head.

The shootings are on the news stations, all the time, which is how I guess the whole world knows. It's like, weather, sniper, sports, sniper, international, sniper, local? No, local means more sniper. Can't they report something different? It's been days since anyone was shot, and I really don't need to think about this all the time, but it's getting to be like a song that's stuck in my head, which is such a crude way of putting something where people are dying, I know, but with the news stories and ads for bulletproof vests and my father's phone ringing again and again, it's not as if I'm the first one making this vulgar.

Li—

I don't know what to say to you. You were really an asshole. You're probably still really an asshole while you're reading this.

I guess D.C. is more important to me not even because of Cody's dad, but because it was D.C. and that was where I was.

But it did suck about Cody's dad. But you didn't know that.

You did know I was in D.C. so you should probably assume that I give a shit about things that happened here.

*Sorry if I insulted New York. But this is your home now, you
know? Wheaton, Maryland, that's yours.*

Craig

He IMs me Sunday afternoon. **This isnt my home. Im
always gonna be from NYC.**

I reply: **From NY yea but not in NY.**

home is where the you know

I guess

So his heart isn't here. I shouldn't be surprised. I mean,
neither is mine, really, right?

And it was only a kiss. God, what would I have done
with his heart, anyway? Knowing me . . .

Before I try to sleep on Sunday night, I give Mrs. Carter
a call. She's got to be so lonely in that house by herself,
no Cody, no husband. When I ran into her at the grocery
store, her cart was practically empty. One tangerine, one
thing of yogurt, one toothbrush, and all those avocados.

"Craig," she says. "How *are* you?"

"I'm fine, you know, yeah, I'm fine. Mostly I'm looking
for all of my animals." And then I tell her about all of the
animals, and she says something about how she doesn't
remember me having all of them back when "she used
to see me all the time," and we both dance around the
subject of why she doesn't see me much anymore and

why the animals are around now when they weren't then. And what it could possibly mean that those animals are no longer around.

Or I dance around it, because I guess she couldn't possibly know most of that. But she makes sympathetic noises in the right places and then she asks me about the sniper, which I guess was what she meant the first time she asked how I was.

She says, "God, I worry about you kids in a time like this. I still remember when JFK was assassinated. I was scarred for years after that."

What does JFK have to do with anything? Maybe she's losing her mind too, and I can't decide if that would be a bad thing, because maybe she and Cody could be together then? Did she know JFK or something?

I say, "I was just wondering if maybe you've heard from Cody lately."

"Yep, he called yesterday. They had a dance at his school; isn't that nice? He sounded like he had a good time."

Oh, God. He met a boy. No wonder he hasn't been emailing. He has some boy and they danced all night like Eliza Doolittle and . . . whoever she danced with.

I say, "That's great. Did you tell him I said hi?"

She says, "Oh, you know what? It might have slipped my mind. I thought you were still talking to him."

"I am." I breathe out. "He hasn't emailed me in a few

days, so . . . yeah. That's why I called, I guess. To make sure he's okay."

Her voice softens. "Aw, honey, I'm sorry. I'm sure he's just been busy. You know, he has a lot to do right now, with his junior year."

She keeps pretending he's in normal school.

"I know," I say. "I didn't call to make you apologize for him, really. I was really just making sure he was okay."

"He's fine," she says. "Cody's fine."

Yeah. "Okay. Thanks. Tell him I said hi?"

She says she will.

Maybe I'll play therapist with myself. Maybe that'll help. I mean, if Cody's all better, and Lio says it helps, I mean, maybe they're onto something.

Cody's happy.

And how do you feel about that?

Really good. I used to do everything I could to make him happy, you know? One time I cranked one of those ice-cream makers by hand for hours and hours because they didn't have mint chocolate chip at the store and that was the kind that he wanted. And his smile made it all worth it. And when he was happy, it was so, so good. So it really is good that he's happy now. That's what I wanted all along. The problem is that he's happy because of a dance, which probably means that he met a new boy.

And how do you feel about that?

Really shitty. I thought we were made for each other. But it's not like I was sitting here waiting for him, or maybe I was, and I don't know if I'm supposed to be, or if I still am.

And how do you feel about that?

Lonely. Bored.

And how do you feel about that?

I feel like this is stupid.

Am I four years old? All I do is cry and say things are stupid.

I'm stupid.

LIO

I'M IN HISTORY ON MONDAY WHEN MY CELL PHONE starts buzzing. Luckily, we're in the middle of a rousing conversation about Rochambeau, so no one hears it vibrate in my pocket.

At that moment, we hear the *bing* of our teacher's email, and he goes to his desk and checks it. He frowns, but he doesn't tell us anything.

The buzz and the *bing* are connected. I know it immediately.

I fake a sneeze and duck into the hallway to fake-blow my nose.

I check my phone. Michelle.

She's already sobbing when my phone connects to hers. She doesn't even wait for me to say hi and then start crying. That's when I realize it's real.

I say, *"Are you okay?"*

And she says, "Thiskidgotshotoutsidemyschool." And then she's sobbing again. My sister. "H-he got shot."

"What?"

"My friend saw it, j-just outside. He j-just . . . he was *about to go inside—*"

She's okay. She's okay. It wasn't her. I still can't breathe. "Holy shit, Michelle. Holy . . . Oh, God, God, fuck."

She mews. "Th-they're going to make me hang up in a second, we're on lockdown."

"Okay. Okay. You called Dad, right?"

I can hear her brush against the speaker of the phone a few times. She's nodding. "He's o-on his way."

"You're safe. You're safe? There are adults with you?"

"Yes." She sniffles.

"Okay. You . . . don't do anything stupid, okay? Stay safe until Dad gets there. Stay safe after Dad gets there!"

I let her hang up first.

I should call Dad. I want to. But he doesn't need to worry about me right now. All my sisters are probably attacking him with calls, or they will as soon as they recognize the name of Michelle's school. Maybe I should call Veronica, my middle sister? She's six years older than me, but she always reads my papers before I turn them in, and she's good at softball, and boys like her. Would she be good at this?

He told us our children were safe at school.

My lungs are tightening up.

He told us they were safe.

My teacher sticks his head into the hallway and says, "Lio."

I'm standing here holding my phone. He could give me detention. I expect him to at least take my phone away.

He says, "Back to class, now, okay?"

My tongue feels too heavy for my mouth. I nod and follow him back inside the classroom, but I don't know if I'm going to stay or if I'm going to get my things and run.

They've rolled out the TV, and everyone's crowded around watching the news. There's the outside of my sister's school. There's a reporter, and her hair is perfect. There's the police chief, and he's crying.

He's crying.

He's our police chief, and he's crying.

I need to get out of here. I need to get to my sister.

I'm fully willing to fake an entire string of sneezes to get out of this class, but the bell goes off as I'm gathering my stuff. Everyone mills around, mumbling to each other.

Thirteen years old. How did this happen?

How the fuck do they think it happened? Exactly the

same as the ones who *weren't* thirteen. Why do we care so much more when it's a kid who dies?

Michelle is fine. She's fine.

I want to go to Craig. I don't know if I can go to Craig. I don't know if we're talking.

So I find Jasper. "We have to go get Michelle."

For a minute I'm terrified no one's told her, and I'm going to have to do it. She'll start to cry. I don't know if I can handle that.

But she puts her arms around me and holds me.

Jasper and I don't touch very much. I hug Michelle a lot more, though I get along more easily with Jasper. But the way we get along tends to be quiet and snarky.

Everyone can see her. A senior hugging a sophomore. I want to bury my head in the shoulder of her puffy jacket and fall asleep.

She says, "Dad's with her, baby. Dad has her."

I know that she's right. But it doesn't feel like enough. I say, "Can we go get the house ready for her?"

She shoves her hair out of her eyes. Her makeup is all smudged. Was she crying? Why haven't I cried? "This isn't a surprise party, Lio."

I pull back from her.

She sighs.

"Give me your keys," I say.

She says, "I know you want to be there for her right now.

But what Dad needs to know is that we're safe and that we're where we're supposed to be. He doesn't need us in his hair right now."

"Keys."

"And I have a test."

"Jasper, give me your fucking goddamn keys!"

She takes them out of her pocket but doesn't hand them to me. "What are you going to do with them? You can't drive. You are *not* driving my car."

I say, "I just need the house key." I'm lying.

"How are you getting home?"

"I'll figure it out!" I run off before she can say anything. I'm faster than she is. But she's not following. Hugging in the halls is one thing, but she isn't going to be seen chasing after me.

I bring her keys to Craig. He's at his locker, fondling the pictures of his animals. Like they're scratch-and-sniff pictures, and they will feel closer to real if he touches them enough.

I say, "Can you drive?"

Craig looks at me for a second. "Are we talking?"

"Please?"

"You're talking." He looks at me, down his nose, like he's doing it to remind me how short I am. How does he do that? How does he make me care? I'm used to being this height. How does he make me feel so small?

He says, "Why are you talking to me? Jesus, what do you want, Lio? I already feel like shit."

I guess I thought . . . the emails . . . I guess I thought we were okay.

He says, "I'm sorry I assumed New York was some kind of haven of personal growth and identity and community wellness or something. Because . . . well, clearly you came from there, so I guess it has to be at least a little—"

"—fucked up," I finish, quietly.

He's really surprised I interrupted him. "Yeah." He clears his throat. "A little fucked up." He looks away and finishes taking books out of his locker. I hope he doesn't cry. I think it's adorable how much he cries, but I can't deal with any more crying today. That's probably why I'm not doing it.

I say, "I need to get home."

He looks at me. "What's up?"

"The kid who got shot goes to my sister's school. I don't . . . I don't think she saw anything. But she's really freaked out. Dad went to get her. I feel like I should be home." I'm panting.

I force the keys into his hands.

Craig puts his hand on my arm and looks down at the keys. "I can't drive."

He showed me his learner's permit the day he got it. He was so proud. I say, "You're better than I am."

He nods a little. "Okay. Come on."

CRAIG

REALLY, I SHOULD CALL MY BROTHER. HE WOULD
pick us up.

But Lio wants me to be his hero.

And I'm really only a little bit mad at him, anymore,
especially since he talked to me, he came to me and he
talked to me, and he asked me for help.

And that's a reminder that I really, really want to be the
one to fix him.

The rain is coming down like crazy, so I'm trying to hurry,
plus Lio looks like he's about to require the use of psychiat-
ric drugs. He leans against the car and blows on his hands

while I unlock it, his collar hitched up so it protects some of his skin from the cold. It's an old car, so both doors need to be unlocked by hand before we can get in, and Lio's just standing there, nursing a cigarette between his fingers, trying to keep it lit, taking short drags on it like they're all he can stand.

He's making a lot of glances over each shoulder—Is anyone coming? Who's coming?—but I tell myself he doesn't want to get caught, not that he's worried he's going to get shot, because I really don't know what to think, if all of a sudden Lio's afraid of getting shot. I don't know what that means about anything.

Anyway, he's not freaking out or anything, he's just a little twitchy.

"Ready?" I ask him.

He gets in the passenger seat and pulls his seat belt on tight. He shakes his head to dry off. He's soaked, which sucks, because he's wearing really nice clothes today. Not nice as in formal, I mean, his black jeans have holes in both knees, but in the way that his hat looks like something he meant to wear and not something he tugged on as an afterthought and his shirt is gray in a way that looks silver.

He shivers while he puts out his cigarette. He should have worn a raincoat like I did, though I wish I'd brought an umbrella instead of a raincoat so I could share it. Once

I get to his house, I'll hold my arm over his head on the walk—probably the run—in, so he won't get any worse.

"You okay?" I say.

He nods. I find the heat and turn it on. He sneezes quietly, and it might be the most adorable thing I've ever seen. It's so stupid, but that sneeze makes me entirely not mad at him anymore. Maybe most of my anger was already gone, or maybe it's the look on his face afterward, staring straight ahead while he emanates waves of *Craig hug me.*

Damn it. I need to focus.

"Can we talk while I do this?" I crank the key in the ignition. "It's just, I mean, I've only driven like twice, and it's kind of hard for me to concentrate when it's all quiet. So if you could talk? Alternately, you can make noises like animals. That'll help."

Lio meows for a minute, and I nearly die from so many feelings.

I ease out of the parking lot. He's stopped meowing by now. I say, "But seriously, talk?"

"You talk," he says. "I'll answer. Promise."

I say, "So are you gay or whatever?" I watch the other cars for a minute to remind myself which side of the road I need to be on. It's not something you think about when you're not driving or when there isn't someone you give a shit about in the passenger seat.

He says, "Yeah."

"I didn't know. I mean, I kind of assumed, but I kept leaving you places to drop it into conversation or whatever and you never did."

"I thought you knew." He pauses, and I try to think of something else to say, and then he says, "I'm sorry."

His voice is so quiet and naked.

I say, "You really made me so mad. And I really just don't feel like being mad, you know? And I don't want to be thinking about all of this, but last night I was thinking that if you ever got sick, it would really freak me out."

He doesn't answer.

I say, "When you sneezed just now, it reminded me, that's all."

"Because of the cancer?"

"Yeah."

"I don't have cancer anymore." I hear him pick at his jeans and I want to check on him, but I need to concentrate on the road. I can see him a little out of the corner of my eye, so I see when he turns toward the window and fusses with his hat in this way that I can tell he doesn't notice he's doing it.

He says, "Every time I get a cold, it's like my dad is holding his breath. Or if I get a nosebleed. Or a bruise."

I don't know what those things have to do with leukemia, but I'm sure they're significant. And I hate myself a little because instead of listening to the feelings behind his words,

I'm keeping a list of these things in my head, inscribing it into myself that I need to watch him if he gets a cold. Or a nosebleed. Or a bruise.

I say, "Can it come back? I mean, I know it can, but . . . I mean, is it something that you need to be worried about or whatever? Or even, like, thinking about?"

"It's statistically more likely that I will get cancer again than that someone who's never had cancer will get cancer. But it's by no means certain or even likely that I'm going to get it again. There's about a seventy percent chance I'm done with leukemia for good."

This is the first thing I've ever heard Lio say that doesn't seem to cost him a lot of effort. He doesn't agonize every word. I can see him well enough to be pretty sure that he doesn't rub his nose while he talks. I realize, a minute of silence later, that this is because it's the first time, I'm pretty sure, I've heard him say something not true. I mean, it might very well be *true*, I don't know. But he doesn't believe it. It's not true for Lio.

I say, "You worry about it?"

He shrugs.

I don't think I ever would have figured that out on my own, without this conversation, without that shrug, even if I knew Lio for a million years. I don't know why I think that, because I'm generally so good at shaking things out of people that they don't want to talk about, that they probably shouldn't be talking about, but I just have the feeling that this is something that Lio is really good, even by his standards, at not talking about. I think this is totally different from the dead brother thing, but maybe the only reason I think that is because he's still picking at his jeans, and when he talks about Theo he's always so calm. It's hard to know. I'm so focused on driving.

I say, "I don't think you're going to get cancer. I really don't think so. I mean, smoking doesn't help, probably, but you're not going to get cancer."

He shrugs again. "If you had been around when I was five, you wouldn't have thought I was going to get cancer then, either. I was just a kid."

And even though I don't think I could have figured out, now, that he's scared, I still think I could have looked at kid-Lio, even if I was five years old myself, and known that he would be one of the kids who gets cancer. I can't get it out of my head that he would have had that old-photograph-cancer-kid glow.

But I've never known a cancer kid in real life. I guess there aren't that many of them. I wonder what the chances are that one identical twin gets cancer if the other one does. I know Lio knows.

He says, "Some five-year-olds have to get leukemia. They just have to. It doesn't matter to cancer which kids."

But it didn't have to be Lio. And it won't be Lio again. I know it.

I want to pull this car over and say all the things we haven't said yet. I want to scream at him, what the fuck is this relationship, what are we doing, why do I care more about you than I do even about my missing animals, why have you gotten your way into my head when I can't have you right now, when I probably can't have you ever because I am a fifteen-year-old torn to shreds, do I just feel this because you're crazy, is it just because you're crazy and I need to fix a crazy boy, is all of this just because I need to fix something and holy mother of God, Lio, can I fix you, and you *better* not get cancer again!

"You missed the turn," he says.

"What?" Fuck. I was driving to my house without thinking about it. I was driving to my house with a kid in the car that I've already decided can't come to my house, what the fuck, Craig, what the fuck.

Lio says, "U-turn?"

"Fuck no, I don't know how to U-turn." I slow to a stop at a red light and look around. I don't see anywhere good to turn.

He shivers a little. "I don't know how else to get there. I don't know this place at all." He curls up with his head in his hands.

And at that moment, that's when I know.

That's when I know as much as I think that I can.

I say, "Come on."

He looks up.

I say, "My house, come on." I keep driving down this road. "You're coming home with me."

He doesn't protest. He doesn't say no no no I need to be with my family.

I'm going to take that as a sign.

The light turns green.

I unlock the front door. "Do you want some hot chocolate?"

He stands there, dripping on the kitchen's fake tile. He takes his hat off and wrings it in his hands. "Really?"

"Of course."

"Where are your parents?"

"At work."

He coughs a little. I say, "Hey. Let me get you some dry clothes."

He comes up beside me, quietly, while I put the kettle on to heat up water. I should probably make it with milk, that's probably better. But the package says water, and I don't want to screw it up.

He says, "I like your house."

"Oh. Thank you."

"Craig?"

I swallow and turn around. And there is Lio, and right now he is all blue eyes and wet hair.

He says, "Do you have two sets of dry clothes?"

"What? Of course. Why?"

He pushes me up against the counter. I'm cold every-where he touches me, except my mouth, my mouth is burn-ing against his mouth. I'm all wet. I'm melting.

Lio meets the animals and says hello to Zippers again. He asks me, softly, if I'd like to go out looking for them tonight. I want to so badly, but he's shaking already from asking me, and I think he's had enough scare for one day. "Maybe someone will call who found one," I say. "Wouldn't that be better?"

He nods.

"Yeah. So someone else can find them tonight."

He looks around the kitchen, the dining room, giving him-self a small tour. I should show him around, or say something, but I'm too stunned by his presence in my house. He fits in like a painting into a gallery, in a way that I never did. I've always been too loud and too messy for my parents' things.

"Where's your brother?" he asks eventually.

"At the mall."

He laughs. "We should hook him up with one of my sisters. They love the mall."

"He's old."

"So are some of my sisters!" He has this huge smile on his face, like he was carved from a pumpkin. When do I ever see Lio smile?

He looks fucking adorable in my pajamas, like he's a kid

on Christmas morning, or a boy trying on his dad's clothes. It's so much easier just to look at him than to think about things, and the truth is that looking at him is making me goddamn happy.

After about an hour—we play video games—I tell him, "You really need to call your dad. And probably your sister."

"Which one?"

"Um, as many as you like, but I was thinking mostly the one whose car you stole."

He nods and uses my house phone and lies on the floor of the living room with his feet up on the table and Michelangelo, who Mom brought home from the shelter, curled up on his stomach. (Still need: One dog, two cats, two rabbits, a guinea pig).

"Hey, Dad," he says after a minute. "How's Michelle?"

He's quiet for a long time. I wonder if his dad is talking this whole time or if there are long pauses where he waits for Lio to speak.

And then he keeps asking about Michelle, again and again, like each time his dad isn't giving him enough of an answer, or isn't giving him the answer he wants. And I remember when we first started talking, over IM.

Liodore: you have siblings?
ThisIsntSparta: a brother

Liodore: how many?

ThisIsntSparta: 1?

Liodore: must be weird

ThisIsntSparta: how many sisters do you have?

Liodore: a million

　see, theyre kinda my whole world

Now I'm sitting here watching him nod at the phone and beg for more information on the sister that he wanted to be with, that he skipped school to be with, and I'm thinking that I should have just made the U-turn. It's no good if I want him to be here more than he does, that's not how this can work. I need more of a push than that. He shouldn't be here. Shit shit shit shit what am I doing?

Then Lio tells his dad, "I'm at Craig's," and I can tell by the way he says my name that he's told his father about me. I feel kind of obnoxiously happy.

"I'm totally safe," he says. "We're right by the school . . ." He closes his eyes for a second. "I know. I know."

He seems smaller than usual when he talks to his father. Not in a bad way, just a younger one. I wonder if everyone gets younger when they talk to their parents. I spend too much time around mine. I need to get out of the house more. I need a hobby. Besides the animals. Maybe I'll start trying to give a shit about karate again.

He says, "Yeah. Craig drove. Yeah, he has his license."

I grin a little. Yeah, okay.

He says, "That's fine. Can she bring me clothes and a toothbrush?"

I look at him. I'm probably making the same face his dad is. *Are you sure? Don't you want to be with your family right now? Don't you want to be surrounded? Aren't you scared? You sound scared.*

"Yeah, I'm sure," he says. He nods. "I want to stay here tonight." His voice is so quiet. "I feel safe here, Dad."

It's not until after he hangs up that he says, "Is that okay?"

"Of course. Um, we have a spare room."

He nods.

"Upstairs," I say. It's not really a spare room. Technically it's actually my room. But I moved to the basement when my dad started worrying about the pee and the carpet. Animal pee, obviously.

Like he's reading my mind, he says, "Where's your room?"

He doesn't ask in a sexy way, just in a curious way. And that makes me feel a little relieved, to be honest. I think, that if we did share a room, I'd be more likely to cry myself to sleep tonight than try anything. It's one of those nights. And maybe Lio is one of those boys.

The stomachache I got when he was on the phone is back, and, God, maybe I really did make a huge mistake, bringing him here, kissing him back, dressing him in my clothes, looking at him in my clothes.

"The basement," I say. "Come on." I lead him down, one hand on the banister, flicking on the lights as I go. I feel bad that his feet are bare. He must be freezing. "Do you want some socks?" I ask.

He shakes his head.

"Come on." I toss him a pair. Then another. "Don't get sick." He only puts on one pair, so I yank the others on my own feet.

He sits on my bed without pausing, like he doesn't even think about the fact that it's my bed—my place, where I stare at the ceiling and jack off and sort of sleep. He sits like he belongs here, like he's decided on his own, and then he leans forward onto his knees and looks around the room.

He wrinkles his nose up. Good thing he wasn't here when it was packed full of animals.

"I know," I say. "Smells like a litter box, yeah I know, because animals sleep down here with me. This is sort of home base for them. That's kind of why my parents stuck me down here. Maybe my brother's glad, because he has the whole upstairs to himself. I think my parents are start-ing to wonder why he hasn't moved out." I don't think I usually babble this much, but I could completely be wrong.

Lio says, "Why?"

"Why are they wondering, or why hasn't he moved out?"

It barely bothers me, having to lead him like this. Maybe it isn't a character flaw. Maybe it's how Lio is. Maybe I should stop trying to fix him.

I shake my head a little.

I don't know what comes after trying to fix him. Or maybe I do, and maybe that's the problem, I really just don't know.

Lio looks at me for a second, then says, "Second one."

"Why hasn't he moved out. Um, I don't know. I think . . ." Maybe I do know. "I think he needs to know that we're okay all the time."

And then Lio says, really softly, "I miss my mom."

I sit down on the bed next to him. And then I'm kissing him because I don't know how to fix him and I think this will help. Or it has to help. He moans really softly, but of course I'm the one who's crying, crying because this kid misses his mom who I don't even know, and how well do I even know the kid? But I know the missing, at least.

I wipe my cheeks off the second he pulls away. I wipe them off hard, like that makes it manlier or something. Lio watches.

"I cry, like, all the time," I say.

He nods. "I know." A smile plays with his mouth. "It's okay. Sometimes I get cancer."

"You're *horrible*," I tell him. But now I'm laughing, big and strong and real like I want to be.

×　×　×

When I tell him he can't smoke inside, he shuffles his feet and chews on his lip for a while before he eventually says, "Okay," and takes a small step out onto the deck. As much as I hate cigarettes and as much as I've worried about his cellular growth today, I kind of like that the clothes he's wearing, my clothes, will smell like them now, and even though I don't understand why he's worried about the sniper, I like that he keeps his palm pressed against the door behind him while he smokes, like a kid keeping his hand on home base during freeze tag. Safe.

LIO

WHEN CRAIG'S PARENTS GET HOME AND ASK WHO I am, Craig cuts in and says, "Lio," with a significant look that makes my heart beat twice when it should beat once. He says something under his breath, probably about my sister. The next thing I know, everyone's hugging. His mom hugs me. Then his dad. They smell like hospitals.

"Are you staying for dinner?" Mrs. Privett asks me.

I look at Craig, but he's cleverly looking away. Damn it, he's going to make me talk.

What's weird is, I'm willing to talk, because I have an unexpectedly intense desire for them to like me.

Christ, I really must love him.

So I say, "Yes, please."

I sit at dinner nicely with Craig's parents and his brother. I can tell immediately that Todd disapproves of me for what's probably some deep philosophical reason I'll never understand, judging by the way he's dressed. I say please and thank you. I pass things when they're requested, and sometimes when they aren't requested but someone seems to be running low. And by someone I mean Craig.

He smiles at me, and for the first time in a while, I feel like I'm doing all right.

Mr. Privett asks him, "How was your day?" and instead of saying "fine," and passing to the next sibling, like I always do at home, Craig says, "You will not believe what happened to me between first and second period," and he starts talking. He tells some long rambling story about a boy who stood too close to him at the urinal.

Todd passes the glazed carrots. I'm sure this is another sign of him quietly hating me. Wasn't choking down the first serving of carrots enough? I try giving him my *I'm fine* smile, but he's not looking at me. I take two or three carrots.

Craig is still telling his story, though I've lost track of what exactly is going on. He's very passionate about it. "And he was all offended, this kid, and he kept asking me if I thought he was a faggot, which was really weird." He pauses and gives a dog who walks up a few good rubs. I palm one of my carrots and offer it to the dog. He/she/it eats it right up. Wow, pets are awesome.

Craig kicks me, so gently. "Listen to my story."

I nod and slip another carrot into my palm. And I am listening. It's just that Craig has a lot of great qualities, but coherency is not one of them.

Craig says, "And he's like, oh, so is that the problem? You think you don't know me, so I must have some disease or something? You're afraid of pissing next to me because I must have some disease, is that it?"

"This is ridiculous," Mrs. Privett says, spearing a green bean on her fork. "I don't believe this."

I feed the dog another carrot.

"No," Craig says, "You have to believe it. You have no choice but to believe, because this is real life. So I'm like, 'dude, I don't know what your problem is, but I'm just trying to pee here,' and he pulls back from the urinal, still . . . well, exposed, and he's like, 'so you think I'm a faggot, is that it!?'"

Mr. Privett goes, "Craig. Do you have to keep using that word?"

"I'm gay, I think I can use it. Faggot faggot faggot. It's what they call cigarettes in Britain, isn't that right, Lio?"

I nod.

Mrs. Privett looks at me all skeptical and motherly. "And how would Lio know what they call cigarettes in Britain?"

I don't know what to say. I cough a little. Todd says, "Getting sick, Lio?"

"No," Craig and I say together.

"Just cold," I say, softly, and Craig gets up from the table.

Mr. Privett says, "So what's up with your hair, kid?"

Craig comes back with a sweatshirt and puts it around my shoulders. "He used to have cancer." I look at him. Are there amphetamines in his water glass? For the first time since I've known him, he might be entirely present.

Although he could also just be panicking. I try to catch his eye, but I can't.

I say, "It has nothing to do with cancer. But it's still, um, kind of a morbid story?"

Mrs. Privett says, "Oh, you don't have to tell us anything you're not comfortable with."

As much as I can tell Craig wants to hear it, what really inspires me to tell this story is looking at Todd. He's scraping his knife around his plate, his upper lip curled inside his lower. He's not listening to me. He still doesn't take me seriously, even though we just threw the word "cancer" around. Does he really think I'm not good enough for his hyperactive little brother? What did I do to piss him off?

Fine. I take a deep breath.

"There's this service online," I say. "You send them a picture of your kid. It's really expensive. They scan it and send you back a folder with the kid at different ages. What he would look like."

Craig says, "So, like, if you're really curious about what your kid's going to look like?"

I give him a look.

Craig says, "Ohhh, so, like, if your kid dies and you're really curious about what he would have looked like?"

I nod. "That one." I rub the back of my head where my hair is growing in unevenly. It's dark red back there, I think, and faded blue in the front. There's also some green, but I can't remember where. Really, I'm blond. "So they sent in pictures of my twin and we got them back and it was . . . scary. To see what he would have looked like. What I'm going to look like. There was a picture in there—THEODORE, AGE 16. I'm going to be sixteen in a month. So I cut it off and dye it lots of colors. Now I don't look like the picture."

"You were a twin?" Mrs. Privett says. Her voice is so soft and gentle, like whipped cream. Whipped cream that feels sorry for you.

I say, "I am a twin."

Craig smiles at me. It's been a long time since I've seen that expression on someone. He is proud.

"More carrots, Lio?" Todd asks, because I'm down to one. I say yes. I'm a doormat.

But I made Craiger proud.

CRAIG

LIO'S DAD DRIVES JASPER OVER ABOUT AN HOUR AFTER dinner. He stays in the car while she comes in, which I can tell Lio doesn't feel right about, because he keeps looking out the window at his dad in the car. "Is he mad at me?" he says eventually. "He didn't sound mad on the phone."

"I don't know. My keys?" She takes them from Lio and hands him a small bag. "Toothbrush and shit."

"Why isn't Dad with Michelle?"

"How the hell was I supposed to get here without him? And she's sleeping in the backseat."

"Oh." He's still peering out the window. I can see his little sister's feet in the backseat. They're in socks and curled up against the window.

Jasper says, "I told him he doesn't get to chew you out about the car when Craig's here. So he thought it'd be best to stay outside. I think I finally got it through his head that Craig's . . . you know."

Lio keeps frowning, but then his dad waves at him, and his face lights like a candle. "Okay."

"Hey." Jasper takes Lio's shoulder and yanks him around. "I didn't say *I* wouldn't chew you out in front of Craig."

I swear he shrinks like five inches.

She says, "You ever do that again, I'll skin ya."

He nods.

She lets her air out and pushes Lio's hair back. "You sure you don't want to come home?"

They're both speaking in these really quiet voices, but it doesn't sound like they don't want us to hear. They're standing in the middle of our kitchen, after all. It sounds like they're being gentle with each other.

Lio nods, looking down.

"We're worried about you."

He shakes his head.

"Do you want to call Adelle?" She takes out her cell phone. She must have his therapist's number in her phone. I bet if I had a therapist, Todd would have her number. I don't need to feel jealous right now.

He says, "No. Really, I'm okay."

"All right." She gives him a big hug. "Michelle's okay too. We love you."

He nods and watches her go all the way down the driveway until she gets into her car. His hand holds on to that bag so tight.

In my bathroom downstairs, he washes his face and brushes his teeth and changes into his own pajamas. He gives mine back, folded neatly. If they didn't smell like smoke, I'd guess they were clean.

I feel like I'm on a sleepover back when I was a little kid, with a friend—usually Cody—and sometimes he'd get homesick in the middle of the night and have to be picked up. I remember praying before we went to sleep that he'd still be there when I woke up. It was sort of a toss-up, but I really hated when he left. And it meant there was always this anxiety hanging in the air before we went to sleep. Will he stay or won't he?

I think I really, really want Lio to stay here, to make it through the night, for us to make it through the night, but I can already feel him slipping away. I think his sister coming was bad for him, because now his mind is back at that house and not here with me. And really there's only room for one of us to be this distant, here, and the last thing I can do is hold on hard enough for both of us.

And we haven't even closed our eyes. We haven't even left for separate rooms. It's barely ten.

He sits down on my bed and pets Sandwich.

To fill the silence, I say, "There's no way we're going to find all of them. It kills me. No matter how many we find, it'll never be all. It's never going to be how it was. There will never be as many."

He says, "Maybe it can still be special even if it's not as much."

There's something significant about this, and I don't know what to do with it.

He clears his throat. "Your brother hates me."

"He doesn't. He's just wary with people he doesn't know. He was sort of trying you out. Like a dog. I'm not sure my dad liked you much, but he's weird, ignore him. He's a principal. Automatically predisposed against people with funny hair." I sit down next to him. "You okay?"

He nods.

"It's just that Todd's protective of me. He just doesn't want me to . . . you know. That again. With Cody. You okay?"

He nods again.

"I know you told Jasper you are. Are you really? Are you worried about . . . do you want to talk about the boy who got shot?"

He's still alive. They found a tarot card by him. Death,

of course. Even I have to admit that's some scary shit. But he's still alive.

He says, "Michelle's safe now. It's like lightning."

"Definitely."

He rubs his eyes.

Kremlin howls at my feet. I say, "Quiet, you. See, this is why you don't want to sleep down here, Lio. They'll all keep you awake. Good thing I don't sleep."

"Can I ask you something?"

I put my hand on top of his head because it feels right. Really, because it feels like he needs it. He's shaking. "Of course."

He's just so little.

He says, very softly, "I wish we were alone in this room right now."

Is that what he wanted to ask me? But that wasn't even a question. I look at Kremlin, and at Sandwich batting at her tail. "Do you . . . want me to put them upstairs?"

"It wouldn't help." He plays with his fingers. "I wish my sister weren't here."

"What?"

"I wish she weren't here in this room right now. With us. Or my brother. Or your parents. Or Cody." I don't like the way he says Cody's name. I hate that I don't like the way he says Cody's name. "Or the sniper. I wish we were alone."

I want to touch him more, but now I don't think he wants it.

He looks up at me. "What are we doing, Craig?"

Fuck.

I say, "It's just that I think it might be too soon for me."

And then we have that conversation neither of us wants to have, because neither of us wants to believe the things I'm saying or to think that they are important, and he has had such a long day and he looks like he's about to fall asleep, and I probably look like I'm about to cry, and we both want each other, I know it, and here we are sitting around telling each other why we can't have each other and all I want to do is be an each other for once.

What does that even mean, "each other"? Each other what?

How is it that he's been pissed on by the universe again and again and again and here he is, eyes blue and wide and right on mine, waiting for me, and he's scared out of his mind by some sniper, telling me that he doesn't care, that he wants to work through all of this with me? How can he do that, and here I am with one bad boyfriend, pulling my hands back into my sleeves and saying *I won't I won't I won't?*

But I would be the thing to break him. I would say the wrong thing or pull at the wrong seams or kiss him at the wrong times or let him get sick and he would fall apart. He would become completely fucked up. I would ruin him. And I cannot do this again I won't I won't I won't.

And we say all the things we both already knew. We still don't know each other very well, what have we shared, a few awkward kisses, a few fantastic kisses, some secrets that we gave up keeping secret from anyone a long time ago? A few arguments and a few funny conversations? A long-buried passion for *Bananas in Pyjamas?*

And so we get it all out, or I get it all out, and he sits and he listens. And I'm saying it all. I'm still in love with Cody, and it's very possible that the only reason I'm interested in Lio is because he is small and in pain and a little fucked up, and we both know it, but we didn't need to say it out loud, and here we are having this conversation. And I can barely hear myself think or hear him be so quiet because there are way too many fucking other people in this room with us, screaming that they're angry or they're thirsty or that they do or don't love me anymore, shaking at the bars on their cages and threatening to break out or in. They're all I can hear. And Lio won't say anything.

I think I will be taking Cody out on everyone around me for the rest of my life.

And every part of me wants this to work but knows I'll hurt him more if I try. I don't think we can date because I don't think either of us could handle a breakup right now, and maybe that is enough reason to stand around with my hands in my sleeves forever and ever.

And so now I've said it all. It's out there in the open. We're not anything. We're barely even friends. We're two boys in one house, back in our own clothes, about to retreat to our own rooms. Except mine isn't even a room, more like a fortress.

But I touch him because I can't help it. And he lets me. And he moans, so quietly, in the back of his throat, and it is so good to hear him make noise, and I want to touch him, and I do, and I'm not talking anymore, and for a second I've stopped hurting him, but every time I pause to breathe or move my hand or look at him my brain starts spinning again and won't stop. And the footsteps upstairs are making me realize that in a minute we're going to have to stop and get separated because my parents are not going to let us sleep in the same room, even if we want to, which we don'tdowant, and I don't want to start something and be interrupted. I don't want him to leave in the middle of something, because I think I would honestly break into pieces, and this is why I cannot do this.

And he starts to go, and then I'm saying, "Lio, please. Lio, let's do this. Let's not do the bad parts and do the good parts. Lio, please, we need to cling right now." Forget that I'm not ready, forget that I'm waiting for some revelation or some epiphany or something to snap in my brain, kiss me, kiss me, kiss me.

He looks at me. "Everything's fucked now."

It doesn't have to be fucked, we just have to *never stop kissing*. I say, "I really, honestly, know. Everything in the whole world is fucked and I really want to give it a try."

He takes a breath. "You just want to fix me." I don't think that I said that bit out loud, but it sounds so true that it makes my stomach curl up, and I feel humiliated for everything I am.

But he didn't say it mean.

I say, "I want to love you." I don't love him. But this is so true. I really, really want to.

"We're fifteen," he whispers.

I say something Cody used to say to me whenever I'd say we were too young and that this couldn't be real: "So, we still have our hearts."

But I don't know what that means. My heart doesn't feel like it's going anywhere. It's trapped in place. I just don't know where that place is.

Lio lies down next to me and rests his head on my chest for a minute.

My heart is here with Lio for a few seconds. Then it's beating funny again. Too slowly.

He whispers, "Go to sleep."

But I don't sleep, I never sleep, and now I'm crying a little from thinking about sleeping, and I'm so sore and so entirely exhausted, and we kiss a little, but I still want to cry, and he says, "Do you want me to sing you a lullaby?"

And it's so beautiful, and afterward he whispers in my ear, "You're going to have to push harder than that to get rid of me."

He squeezes my hand.

He says, "I'll see you tomorrow."

But now he's gone.

C—

I hope you know how badly you've fucked up my life.

Can you just email me back? Like, I know it's three in the morning and you're probably asleep, but what the fuck, why did you stop emailing? Fuck you, Cody. Fuck you.

You know maybe someday I want to have a real relationship, did you ever consider that? That at some point I might want something in my life that doesn't revolve around this never ending cycling fucking fear that the guy is going to die any second, of a gunshot wound or a fucking self-inflicted gunshot wound or of grief or of cancer. Maybe I actually want to move on from our little fucking eighth-grade whatever and actually because Jesus how fucking lame is it but no matter what I still want you.

I'm not moving on because I want you. And I'm not getting over you because I don't know what the fuck happens after I get over you and I don't want to be left here alone again, okay? Maybe maybe I want someone to stick around, because being the one left behind fucking blows, and I get that it's not like you're having an easy time either, but you should at least have the decency to answer my emails, because it's thanks to me that you're even at that school and not dead right now, did you even think of that? Did you ever thank me for taking care of you all that time?

I love you, you fucking idiot, and I love you crazy and I love you sane, so will you please answer my emails? That's all I'm asking from you, I'm not asking for your love or your brain or your fucking future although, let's be honest, I'd take them all, I'd take them all and I'd keep them safe, just like I'll keep you safe even though I don't think I'm supposed to have to do that, I don't think that's how relationships work, one person taking care of the other one all the time, but damn it I'll do it, Cody, but you have to answer my emails. You fucking have to. Fuck you, Cody, answer me. ANSWER ME. I JUST FUCKED EVERYTHING UP FOR YOU AND YOU WILL NEVER EVEN CARE.

Love,
C

× × ×

I don't sleep.

I don't sleep.

Breathless, awful, impossible, I don't sleep.

I don't sleep.

LIO

I KNEW IT WASN'T GOING TO WORK OUT. AND I KNEW
why, too. Because I'm Cody-lite. When there's still the
possibility, no matter how small, of Cody-real, what am I
good for?

This mattress is hard and rubbery. I can't get it out of
my head how much this room smells like him. And cat pee,
a little, but it really smells like him.

I need to move on. The problem is, I don't know anyone
else. Even before I moved, Maryland meant Craig.

This is so pathetic. Maryland so far has been a boy who
doesn't love me, homework, and six dead bodies.

God, I sang him a lullaby.

I can't believe that. I don't sing for anyone but my dad anymore, and only then when he's drunk after some work party and his *L*s sound like *Th*s and songs come pouring out of me before I can stop them, like some kind of battle cry.

Adelle would have a field day with me right now. Maybe I should start seeing her three times a week now that I'm in love.

I think once you start going to therapy three times a week, you've made some sort of terrible transition. I think that's the difference between "a little fucked up," in a concerned, endearing tone and "fucked up" with raised eyebrows and a slow head nod.

Craig would probably like that. It probably brings me closer to turning into Cody.

That isn't fair of me to think, but I don't care right now.

Maybe all that bullshit about how you never forget your first love is true. Maybe Craig will go through his whole life taking little wounded puppies and trying to mold them into a Cody that he can save. Maybe that's what happens when you get your heart broken.

But I'm *not* just some wounded puppy. I'm not. And I'm not going to let some boy make me all about things that happened to me because that's how he knows how to see me. Shitty things happened to me, and they happened, and I'm dealing. I'm fine with being wounded, but not to prove a point. I'm not an archetype. I'm fifteen fucking years old.

I sit up and look out the window. It's stopped raining now, and the moonlight's glaring through the tree branches. The dark is so heavy that I don't think it can be disturbed. Maybe that's why there haven't been any overnight shootings. The night would muffle gunfire like a pillow.

I want to wrap myself in the dark and disappear.

I want to wrap myself in Craig and disappear.

Will I give in to this? Is my heart broken now? Will I spend my whole life trying to turn boys into him? Dressing them in polos and pricking their fingers to make them cry?

I have a desperate urge to get what I deserve, for once.

I go into the bathroom and drink water out of the sink. It's hard to swallow. My lips still feel tingly, and so does my body everywhere he touched me. Maybe I'm dying.

Tonight, I've been so worried about getting sick again. My whole head is throbbing *cancer cancer cancer*, and I'm paranoid it means something. I got blood work done last month, and I was fine. But I'm scared. I'm scared again. I close my eyes and do deep breaths.

I bet Craig never thinks, "I'm dying."

And to be honest, I probably spend more time thinking, "I'm living."

I sit down on the toilet. I can see myself in the mirror. This is so weird. Who wants to look at themselves in the mirror when they're on the toilet? I guess it's okay when you're only sitting here, like I am now. But I still like to know where mirrors are before they sneak up on me.

I look at myself for a while.

I try it a few different ways; I turn my face at different angles, and push my hair back off my forehead, trying to see how I'd look if I were a tiny bit different in a few different ways.

I am so pathological.

I feel like I need some sort of hotline right now. Not a suicide hotline, more like the opposite. Is there a hotline for people who feel a little too motivated to be alive?

I don't want to die, but I wish waking up every morning didn't feel like such a *fuck-you* every single time. Sometimes I don't want to get out of bed with my hands in fists and a fight song in my throat because rah rah I beat cancer. Sometimes I'm only getting up to go to school, and that has to be okay. I need to calm the fuck down about still being here, but I don't know how.

I'm worried I'm going to go through my whole life feeling like someone's pulling me, like from a string behind my belly button. I'll keep going if you let go. Really. You don't have to make me. I have every intention of sticking around. I didn't *mean* to be ephemeral. I wasn't trying to scare you.

I put my hand against my reflection for a second, like it's a door I can fall through. This isn't *Alice in Wonderland.* I'm not nearly pretty enough. I'm probably not even fucked up enough.

There's a scratching at the door. I open it, and a little white kitten comes in.

I go down the stairs.

I go down the next flight of stairs.

I'm in Craig's room. Or his basement, anyway.

He's on his side on his bed, facing away from me. He's whispering. His voice is so quiet it makes my ears hurt to listen. Maybe whispering for him is like crying for most people.

He says, "Please please I would have saved him if I could, I would have done anything, would have given up anything just to keep him here so that my boy could be okay. I know there's nothing I can do but I need it to be enough that I would have done it, and I need that boy back with me right now."

I can't listen to this without wanting to believe it's about me. I can taste crying in the back of my throat and in my sore mouth. I don't want it.

A dog barks and Craig starts to roll over. Fuck. I run back up the stairs with my six-minute-mile legs.

I hear, "Lio?"

I'm already gone. I sit in a chair in the kitchen. He doesn't come after me.

I whisper, "What if someone breaks in and tries to kill me? What if you wake up and I'm gone?"

I take the phone off the wall and call home. My dad answers almost immediately. And instead of saying hello, he lists all of us who aren't there, top to bottom: "Talia Rachel Veronica Lauren Lio?" He always does that. Always. And it always breaks my fucking heart.

"The last one."

"Honey. You okay?"

"Can you come pick me up?"

"I'll be there in a second."

"I want to come home," I whisper.

CRAIG

WHEN I WAKE UP, HE'S GONE.

I can't say I'm that surprised.

Was that a dream? Did I sleep?

My mom says, "Where's Lio?"

"Left early."

I made his escape too easy. The code for the alarm system is still on a Post-it on the wall, because we can't remember it yet, and clearly my dogs don't give a shit if someone comes or goes in the middle of the night, and I didn't do anything to encourage him to stay, so what did I think would happen? I don't even care that he left, pretty much. It's not like he's dead.

I make myself a bowl of oatmeal. Mom's standing at the counter, reading the newspaper. "Anyone get shot?" I ask.

She clicks her tongue a little. "No."

"Cool."

She says, "You don't need to rush. You're not going to school today."

"Wait, what?"

"We're pulling you out until—"

"Until what?"

"Until this has passed, Craig. God, after what happened to that poor boy, you should be relieved to stay home."

The truth is, I'm not particularly dying to go to school, but somehow I know this means I'm not going to see Lio today, and that sucks.

"Are you still going to work?" I ask, and then, "Is Dad going to work? What's even going on in this house, God, is Todd asleep?" And when all of those are yes, I sit patiently and wait for Mom and Dad to leave and then, woosh, I'm out looking for animals. I find Carolina, my rabbit, scratched but okay, and Mom calls from work and says she has amazing news, that she got a call from the animal shelter and she's coming home with Marigold.

I know that it's amazing, and I try to get as excited about this as I was when we found Sandwich. But I'm having a hard time feeling anything today. It's like I'm finally too tired for all of this.

Two cats.

One rabbit.

A guinea pig.

That night, while I'm hitting refresh over and over, a message finally comes in.

My heart stops and holds midbeat.

C—

Ok ok stop freaking out. I'm fine.

I miss you too.

My shrink told me to stop emailing you.

I heard about the shit happening back home. That's insane. You're safe, right?

Love,
C

Oh, God, he didn't say "Fuck you."

My fingers are going to fly off from typing so fast.

C—

I'm fine. Of course I'm fine. I'm emailing you, aren't I?

Cody, I'm sort of dying without you. You should see the boys I'm turning down because I'm still hung up on you. What's going on over there?

Love,
C

While I'm typing that, my email dings as a new message comes in.

Craiger—

I want to apologize for leaving last night. And for creeping into your room. Basically I'm just sorry for being such a creeper all the time.

School was lame. Hope you enjoyed your day off and you didn't get shot or anything. Oh, sniper humor. Have you watched the news? They're doing all these videos about how to not get shot when you're pumping gas. Informative.

Duck if you see a white van. Or if you're pumping gas. Better yet, don't pump gas, okay? But if you do, you bob around a lot and try to stay behind your car. Thank me later, when you're still alive. Stay alive, Craig, okay? Don't get cancer.

So I don't know what decision we came to, last night, really, and I'm confused, so . . . here's what I think is going to work out best for you. Here it comes.

Essentially, I'm not going to bother you anymore. I don't mean this in like an emo way, though it probably sounds that way to you. I wouldn't blame you for thinking that. You haven't seen much of my ability to make friends. But I swear I can do it. I had a whole posse of gay boys in New York. And I think my father might still think I'm straight. I don't even think he's trying to deny it, I think he really is just that clueless. So he'll probably match me up with a nice Jewish girl soon, and there's a friend.

Anyway, I'm not even sure if there are any fabulous Jews or homosexuals at our school, but rest assured that if there are, I will find them. By Friday they will be my babies. Mark it.

Lio

God, Lio. What am I going to do with him?

I resist the urge to open his email up next to Cody's

and compare them. I know which email is better. I know which boy I . . . I think I know which boy I want. So it doesn't matter.

I sleep.

I dream about Cody.

I wake up feeling dizzy and sick at five in the morning and go upstairs for more food—more food solves everything. And even though there wasn't a shooting all day, I'm not going back to school, my parents tell me. Because obviously no shooting yesterday means there has to be a shooting today. Exactly like whenever there's a shooting it means there's going to be another right after. My parents have gone crazy.

Dad is going to a meeting with some other principals or the school board or something, and his hands are shaking around his tie. Today they're figuring out if they're going to close the local schools.

I notice for the first time this note by the phone, folded up with my name on it. How long has it been there?

And inside is the world's smallest smiley face.

LIO

I'M GETTING PRETTY FUCKING SCARED OF GOING TO
school. In the car, I ask Dad, "I'll go today, but can I stay
home tomorrow?"

There are teachers lined up outside the school to make
sure I don't get shot on my way in.

He takes one of my hands and squeezes. "Yeah, champ.
If it makes you feel better."

Michelle hasn't been back since it happened. A lot of
the kids from her school haven't, I think.

No Craig at school, not that I'm supposed to be looking
for him. Second day in a row. And today is the one-week
anniversary of realizing I'm in love with him. Yay, my life.

I celebrate the occasion by attending a Gay-Straight Alliance meeting after school, before therapy. I told my dad this morning that I was going. He nodded and said, "Have fun." I'm so confused about what he wants me to be and who he thinks I am.

Everyone mills around, waiting for the meeting to start. There are a few flamboyantly gay guys, who I envy and fear at the same time, and some girls in black buckled boots and eyeliner with really long hair.

This is my first GSA meeting ever. And I'm here for the sole purpose of picking up boys. Hopefully a few of them. I need one to make out with, but I would also like a posse.

But more girls come in, dominating the meeting, and there are only three boys who don't scare the fuck out of me. My radar immediately locks on one—Jack Johannson, he says, when we go around introducing ourselves. Alliterative first and last names are my favorite. Like Peter Parker or Ben Bruckner. Amazing.

We talk about dental dams and this talent show coming up and gender-queerness, which is a concept that I want to understand but don't, yet. I sit and listen and don't talk. Afterward, we mill around and eat chips and soda. I am the only one who doesn't drink diet. I love gay boys so much.

I make a beeline to Jack and give him my *I'm short and isn't it cute?* smile. Can I do this without talking?

Apparently so. He smiles at me and holds out his hand. "That'll get you far. What's your name, kid?"

I shake his hand. "Lio."

"Like Tolstoy."

"Uh-uh. L-i-o, short for Liam. Which is short for William."

"A nickname of a nickname."

I missed being teased. Craig is too nice to do it. "Can't get much more abbreviated than that. Soon I'll just be a thoughtful pause." This is an old joke, so it isn't hard to get out.

He laughs a little. "I haven't seen you here before."

"I'm new. Transfer."

"How are you liking the meeting? Are you a freshman?"

"Hey. Sophomore."

He grins and sips from his cup. "Sorry, sorry."

"You?"

"Senior."

Ho buddy.

He takes an Oreo off the table and looks around. Damn. It must be my turn to talk. Um . . . shit. Okay. I say, "So, do you come here a lot?"

He says, "My best friend actually founded the group. Her name is Leah, funny enough." He gestures toward her. She's one of the girls in boots.

I say, "Hey, that's like me," in a dry voice, because clearly that's the point. He laughs.

He says, "Yeah, she and her girlfriend were getting some shit written about them in the bathrooms. It was completely cliché and disgusting. We never thought we even needed a GSA branch here, but there you go. And the school was surprisingly open to it, and I think it's been helpful."

"You're straight, aren't you?"

He chuckles in that way again. "Yeah, I put the S in GSA."

I snap my fingers like, "damn it."

He's still smiling. "I'm too old for you anyway."

And then he gives me a hug.

He asks me how I'm coping with freshman year. I make a face and hit him. Then he asks how I'm coping with the shootings. I give him my usual one-word answers, but he says, out of nowhere, "You're used to saying a lot with your eyes, aren't you?"

It scares me, being noticed. But I nod. Because I like that I didn't have to play the dead brother card or the cancer card for him to understand that there's stuff I'm not saying.

Sometimes, it's nice to remember that I have stuff I'm not saying.

Maybe I'm not as talked out as I thought.

Because there are things I should have said last night when Craig was telling me that he wasn't ready, and telling me that *I* wasn't ready.

I should have said:

It's up to me whether I'm okay with the possibility of being broken.

Plus, I'm a tough little son of a bitch, and don't you forget it.

If you really don't want to be with me, you cannot slide out of it sideways. You have to mean it.

Tomorrow is the one-week anniversary of realizing I'm in love with you.

I catch my breath.

I should have said something. And this is maybe the first time I have ever really meant that.

Jack says, "You okay?"

"Thinking about a boy."

And then Jack makes me talk about Craig. And I do.

I tell him everything.

"Yeah," Jack says. "You need to fight for this boy."

And then he tells me about his ex-girlfriend, and we get more chips.

Eventually, Jasper calls me and says she's here to bring me to therapy. I tell Jack I have to go spill my issues to a paid professional, and he says, "All right, frosh—"

"I'm a sophomore!"

"—get moving. I'll watch from the window and make sure you're safe."

And he does. He really does. He goes upstairs with me, and I look back while I'm walking—running—to Jasper's car. He waves.

I feel really good about all of this, but it's not much to brag about to Craig.

That evening, after therapy, there's another shooting. A guy gets shot while pumping gas.

It seems so awful and surreal. Couldn't he have been doing something else? *Anything* else? Didn't he watch the news? Is anyone but me and the fucking sniper watching the news?

We're safe at school. We're safe at the gas station. So where the fuck are we really safe?

Jack IMs me. I tell him I'm scared but not any more scared than I feel like I'm supposed to be, and he says: **good. u hold on. C u tomorrow, freshman.**

I have a friend. I really do. And he's really my first friend in Maryland, in a lot of ways, because Craig doesn't IM me.

And I don't know if it's because he doesn't care about the sniper, or because he doesn't care about me.

So I open up a chat window for him.

I start a conversation. It's not the conversation we need to have, but it's something.

He deserves that.

CRAIG

I'M HAPPY FOR THE KID AND EVERYTHING, BUT REALLY, how the fuck does Lio get a friend before me? I live here.

told you i could do it :) Lio IMs me. I want to rip out that smiley's eyes.

But I just say, **you're awesome.**

More importantly, how did I get through more than a year at this school without it bothering me that I have no friends?

Oh, right: Cody.

Oh, right: Lio.

I don't really feel sorry for myself. After all, it's all my fault. And the truth is, I could have friends if I wanted them, but I don't really want them. Honestly, if I could be friends with anyone in the world right now, and this sounds really stupid, it wouldn't be the kids in the cafeteria who are so charmed they even get their food for free, or that junior girl who everyone says is *really hot,* or Mansfield or anyone else in my karate class. I think I'd choose my brother.

But he doesn't have time for me.

So I guess I feel a little sorry for myself. And that night I realize I've started spending more and more time outside, standing there, volunteering. Not to get shot. I'm not going to get shot. But I'm all right with welcoming the possibility of something happening. To me. Anything.

To me instead of to Cody instead of to Todd instead of to Lio.

Because a part of me is nervous for him that he went to GSA alone, that he had to talk to people he didn't know, that he didn't have backup, that he was probably scared, and even though nothing bad happened and it's over, I am still nervous, and this is one of those lines again that I am not supposed to cross.

I have to find my animals. I have to find them. Every single one. A lady calls who found a cat a while ago and just saw one of my posters and thinks it might be Zebra. She sends me a picture.

Sometimes I believe in angels.

One cat.

One rabbit.

A guinea pig.

Slowly, they're still trickling home. But I know there's going to be a day when the trickle will

stop

and then no more animals.

But until then.

Craig—

Hope you're doing SWELL. Can we bring "swell" back?

Lio

This is a stupid email and it's *stupid.* And I'm stupid.

And stupid Lio is stupid, too. And his hot friend. Well, I haven't seen him, but Lio doesn't seem the type to make friends with ugly people. I'm going to tell myself that Lio is really shallow. Shallow shallow Lio.

Yeah. Sure.

Lio's tragic flaw isn't that he's shallow, it's that he's . . .

God, I don't know.

I need to stop acting like I know the boy.

It's just a few IMs and a kiss.

His tragic flaw is that he is a walking tragedy, and his smile makes me feel alive.

Friday morning, another guy dies pumping gas. Mom comes home that night and says she didn't remember putting gas in the car, but the tank was full. Todd doesn't make eye contact, but she hugs him hard, then smacks him and tells him he's stupid. I feel like an intruder.

Mansfield has a girlfriend. Her name is Chelsea. Chelsea and Mansfield. He talks about her through our entire karate class, and between kicks, he's telling me how they got to third base in the back of the bus under the cover of his ski jacket.

"It was so hot," he says. "Hot and wet."

I say, "I'm surprised you even ride buses." I try not to sound jealous that he's still going to school. "Are the windows made of bulletproof glass?"

"Ha ha ha. Seriously, you have no idea what it's like. It's like . . . Christmas."

"Third base is Christmas?"

"Pussy is Christmas."

Ew. I hate that word. Like girls have animals in their pants or something. I have no desire to know what girls have in their pants but I do really hope none of it is alive, and I don't think even newborn kittens in a girl's pants could make me go down there. This is so gross. Why am I still thinking about this? I hate karate.

Afterward, when I'm safely in my mom's car where no

bullets can ever get me, Mom pulls up at our house and says, "Is that Lio?"

Yes, that's Lio. He's standing at my door, shaking a little, looking around nervously. I give him a quick hug, and his heart's beating so fast. "You okay?"

He nods.

"Did our car scare you?"

He nods again.

"Shit, I'm sorry."

I scared him.

What is he doing here?

He says, softly, "Jasper had to drop me off. She couldn't wait."

"Oh, um, okay." I let him into the house. "Here. I'll get you something to drink."

Now that he's inside, he's calming down. He takes off his jacket, and his skin is that plain ghost white, his collar too high to show the scar on his chest, and his skin is probably fifteen shades lighter than mine, and I know there are a shitload of people in the world with lighter skin than mine and it's really nothing I'm generally excited about or anything, but his feels sort of like a miracle right now, I can't explain it. It's just that every single thing about him is a miracle.

And something just broke open inside of me, seeing him here, at my table, in his jacket in his skin in my house in my head exactly how I pictured him, making me feel alive even though he isn't smiling, exactly as gorgeous as I remembered he was, and he is here he came back, and my car scared him but I *didn't.*

I did not scare him away, I wasn't too crazy or too needy and he came *back.*

And he starts to say, "I left my hat here," but he has to say the last few words against my mouth because I cannot believe how badly I have to kiss him. I'm kissing him in the kitchen in front of my mom. I'm such an idiot.

But it feels right.

It's not our first kiss, and it's not our first good kiss, but it's the first one that feels right.

And we keep going until Mom clears her throat.

We're in my basement again. We're having the same talk, but different, because this time Lio is talking too.

He says, "I've been talking to Jack all day. He says I'd be crazy not to fight for you. Gloves are off."

I'm saying, "I really like you. I'm still in love with Cody."

"I know you're still in love with Cody."

"I'm not sure how or when that's ever going to stop."

"Okay."

"But this is my life and, who knows, we could get shot any minute."

Lio nods. "Or get cancer."

"Or get cancer. Except not you." And I put my arms all the way around him. I don't love him because he's little anymore. I love him including he's little.

Fuck, I didn't mean to say love.

It wasn't out loud, but I get the feeling he heard it anyway.

And that's okay right now. I love him including loving Cody, and I love him including loving him.

Lio talks. Lio talks a lot. This is so incredibly weird.

"I didn't go to school on Friday," he says.

"Yeah, neither did I."

"My dad says I don't have to go back until I'm ready. I think Adelle wants me to go, but she says I should do what I'm comfortable with."

I keep touching him, his cheek, his back, the scar on his chest, to make sure he's still Lio.

Then I swallow and say, "Are you talking because of Jack?"

He shakes his head. "I'm talking because I wanted to talk about you." He grins. "And now I'm talking to you."

He tastes like Lio.

Lio Lio Lio. I want to say it forever. I could whisper it to him while he falls asleep. I am full of stupid thoughts like this.

"Look how many more animals you have!" He touches every single one he can get his hands on. He has to ask each one of their names about twenty times, but I don't mind. My parents do too.

"Hey hey hey, do you want to go outside and look some more?" I ask. I'm so excited I'm nearly bouncing. "I'm sure there are more still out there, probably they're sensing the ones that have come home and they're on their way. We could go get them!"

But the way he looks at me makes me wish I hadn't said anything. God, he's scared. What is he so scared about? Isn't he the one who taught me about odds? What are the chances, out of all the people in the Maryland-D.C.-Virginia metropolis, we'll be the ones to be shot?

A few days ago, he was the one to suggest we go outside. And I was the one who told him we didn't have to.

Today he says, "Okay."

"I'm going to New York on Monday," he says when we get to the top of the hill.

I look at him. He's not looking at me.

"For just a few days." He keeps rubbing his nose and looking at the ground. I want to shake the words out of him. Gently.

"Why are you going to New York?" I say.

"My mom."

"Your mom's still in New York?"

He nods.

"I didn't know that."

"Yeah," he says. "Dad thinks if I'm going to not go to school, I should at least be taking care of Michelle. And she really wants to go. I guess . . . I don't know. I guess Michelle's thinking of going to live with her long-term. I guess she doesn't feel safe here."

"What about you?" My voice sounds stupid and too small for me.

He looks at me. "Craiger, it's just a visit." He touches my hand. "I promise. I'll be back."

"You better be."

"I'm not going anywhere."

We find Hail, my last rabbit, and he's dead, and something has picked him apart a little. His eyes are closed. He looks like it hurt.

God damn it. My chest hurts.

"Shit," Lio says, softly.

But I take a deep breath, and I'm the one who says, "It's okay. Look, it's going to be okay."

"Sleep upstairs with me?" he begs. "Your parents won't know."

I shake my head. "They're light sleepers."

They're not. They slept through a fucking burglary, for God's sake.

It's just that the thing is that the last time I slept in that bed, I was with Cody.

No, I wasn't, but I was still crying about how Cody was gone and how I was never, ever going to be able to deal.

And I don't want to think about Cody tonight. Even though I think about Cody every night. Even though as soon as Lio leaves the room, I'm going to hit refresh on my email and beg Cody to talk to me. I'm going to fall asleep with his name on my brain.

Lio kisses me good night.

I don't sleep.

Sunday morning, Lio leaves to go home and pack. He gives me a big hug and hands me a note, folded like the last one.

"I'll see you in a few days."

"Of course."

But I can't fix this gnawing feeling in me that this is the end of something, that this weekend we were playing house and now we are back to real life, back to New York and ex-boyfriends and snipers.

I wait until he's gone to open the note.

CRAIG

On the inside, a very small heart.

Home is where the . . . well, you know.

LIO

MICHELLE HOLDS MY HAND LIKE I'M HER MOM IN A
supermarket. This would be okay, except Michelle looks
old for her age and I look young. So people probably think
we're dating. Ugh.

We pass the enormous blue crab statue and stand in line
to go through the metal detectors so we can get x-rayed and
inspected and prodded and studied and excavated and all
that. Security takes a million years longer than it used to.
I have to take off my hat.

The TSA guys are all giving me funny looks. Do I really
look like a terrorist?

I guess no one knows what a terrorist looks like anymore.

Maybe leaving is a mistake. I give Michelle's hand a quick squeeze. It was more for me than for her, but she clings in a way I didn't expect.

She puts her bag on the conveyor belt and steps through the metal detector. I keep watching her until she's all the way through. When we get to the gate, she sits down and wrings her hands.

"Are you worried about the flight?" I say. We haven't flown in so long. But driving from New York to Maryland is, we discovered on the move, sort of a bitch. And not an endearing bitch like Craig.

She shakes her head.

My phone buzzes, and I check the number. Jack. I hit ignore. We're boarding any minute, so I dig a pen out of my pocket and write CALL JACK on the inside of my arm.

"Look who's so popular all of a sudden," Michelle says. She's still attacking her hand with her other hand.

I say, "You okay?"

"I want to get out of here. Like, now. Right now. I want to get the fuck out of Washington, D.C., and back to New York."

This is Maryland. "I know."

She says, "We haven't seen Mom together since . . . what, Christmas?"

"Yeah."

Michelle doesn't say anything else about that, and neither

do I. She shivers and pulls her jacket around herself. Why do they make airports so cold?

I look out the window. It's already dark, and we won't land in New York until almost eleven. All the lights outside come from the flashing bulbs on airplane wings. They remind me of the candles we put in the windows during the holidays.

On the TV mounted to the wall, pretty news reporters are teaching us about Halloween safety without even mentioning there might be a rogue gunman still on the loose when the thirty-first rolls around, and then what are we going to do?

Every day I think, *this is the day they're going to catch him.*

But maybe they never will. Maybe the shootings will just taper out until there are no more. Like Craig's animals.

And we'll never know, and that will always bother us, but it'll be better than getting shot, or than living in fear of getting shot. Or will we always worry that one day he's going to come back? It would be really nice to end this, officially. But I don't know if real life works that way.

The more I think about it, the more I think that catching the guy sounds like some fairy tale I should have outgrown a long time ago.

My father said the two gas station shootings were the sniper saying fuck you to the news reports. Those were why he suggested I disappear for a little while. I don't think he's afraid I'm going to get shot, but he's a little scared I'm going to go crazy from worrying about it all the time. I don't know why everyone assumes I'm going to go crazy at the drop of a hat. It's not like I'm in therapy because I had a nervous breakdown over losing a toy. But I guess I haven't been as zen about the sniper as I would have liked, or expected.

To be honest, I don't even know how I feel anymore. Tired. Scared. Tired from being scared. Grateful to be getting away.

I miss Craig.

Michelle says, softly, "I had a dream about Theodore last night."

I glance at her as the news report suddenly shifts. Someone's been shot. Michelle says, "Shit." I turn back and watch too, my fingers snapping shut around hers.

It was in Arlington, Virginia. That's really close to D.C., but besides that, all I know is that there's a huge army cemetery. JFK is there. The woman was an FBI agent, and she's dead. I hope they bury her there.

God, what do I care if they bury her there? What will that fix?

Adelle would say, *what are you really thinking?*

Everyone in the terminal seems to have squished closer to each other since the news changed from Halloween to real monsters. One hundred heads cocked toward the screen, two hundred hands clutching a bag or a coat or a boarding pass or another person.

All because of one woman none of us knew.

One woman is not very many. Nine dead people, total, is not very many.

But my stomach hurts so hard.

Michelle gives my hand a pull. "We're boarding," she says. Her voice is shaking. "Come on."

I call Craig before takeoff. Even though they haven't made the announcement to turn off electronics yet, the flight attendant watches me, like she thinks I'm going to try to continue this call all the way to New York.

He says, "Lio?"

"Uh-huh." Can he even hear me? I feel so quiet.

Michelle reads the crash instructions from the seat pocket. I'm in the window seat. She has some fat man next to her.

He says, "Lio, is everything okay?"

"Have you seen the news?"

I hear the *click-whump* of his TV. He sighs a little. "Sucks."

"I just wanted to make sure you're okay."

"It was in Arlington, Lio."

"I know . . ."

"Oh, kid." He breathes out. I kind of like when he does this. I love Crazy Craig, but I love Responsible Craig too. He says, "Don't worry, okay? I'm in the basement with Casablanca, about to go searching some more because the sniper is far far far away. Are you okay? You sound way shaken up."

"I'm fine."

"Are you in New York?"

"No, my plane's about to take off."

"I miss you."

Something about the fact that he asked me if I was in New York, and I'm not in New York, and then he says he misses me even though I'm here, I'm just not here *with him* . . . I think I understand for the first time what it means to be in a relationship.

"I'll be home soon," I say, and then we have to hang up. Closing the phone makes my chest twinge so hard I wince.

"You okay?" Michelle says.

"I miss him."

She rolls her eyes. "You'll see him in, like, a minute."

"I don't like leaving him here."

She shrugs and turns a page in her magazine. After a minute, she says, "You're the one always saying the chances are miniscule."

And for the first time in my life, words come out of my mouth before I can agonize over them. Before I even hear them at all.

I say, "But this is Craig."

I feel something turning in my head like clockwork.

Craig is just one person. The chances that he will get shot are the same as anyone else's.

The hole in the world when he's gone would be the same size as the FBI agent's.

Except . . .

It wouldn't be.

To me.

I have no way to measure these holes.

Click.

Numbers don't matter.

Because what if loss is immeasurable? What if all we can do is call a loss a loss?

What if the FBI agent is worth as much as Craig? What if my brother is worth as much as September 11th?

There is no way to measure these holes.

One dead person today is one person who is dead, one whole person who is not around anymore, and that's horrible. And now, nine dead people are dead forever and ever. That isn't less than September 11th. It can't be. Because how could you ever figure out how many people it takes to equal one person?

Nine people and three thousand people and one hundred eighty-nine people are all numbers that shouldn't have happened. But they're not enough to measure a tragedy. We're not just numbers. Someone loves us.

I want to get off this plane, but it's taking off. I'm breathing too hard. I haven't been on a plane in three years.

"Hey." Michelle squeezes my hand. "You're okay."

Did planes always feel like roller coasters? I don't want to crash I don't want to crash. I don't want to die.

CRAIG

CRAIGER—

At Mom's apartment now. It's small and smells like cats, a smell I have become familiar with recently.

The weird thing is, Mom doesn't have any cats.

She's about the same. DEAD BROTHER came up in conversation and she so obviously danced around him, it was pathetic. The sick thing is that I think she's doing it for me. If it were too painful for her to talk about, that would be one thing. But it's as if she doesn't know I've been dealing with this for seven years. Shockingly, my life continued when she (and the kid himself, too) wasn't here. Whatever.

Any new animals?

Say hi to Todd for me. Maybe throw in something about how I make you deliriously happy and there's no reason for him to hate me. I dunno, up to you.

Just wanted to let you know I got in all right. And also that my chest hurts as if I MAY BE DYING, because I accidentally left my heart on your kitchen counter. I hate when that happens.

Li

———————

C—

Craaaaaigor. My school's having an open house on Saturday. I guess they want to prove to our parents that we're not being electroshocked. Come?

Love,
C

My inbox smells like conflicting feelings and guilt.

Also, why does Lio spell "Craiger" with an -er and Cody spell it with an -or? That's weird.

The fact is, I'm going through all our conversations again and again, and I'm pretty sure that Lio and I never made anything official before he left. I wish we had.

"Mom?" I say.

She's sewing. She only sews when she's stressed. She's shoving her needle through the cross-stitching fabric like she's trying to kill it.

She's watching the news, even though it's Wednesday and no one's been shot since Monday. I told Lio this was a really shitty week to choose to leave, considering the lack of death, so much lack that my parents are actually considering sending me back to school, and he IMed me back with a laugh I could read—**im not here to escape anything.** I'm not fooled, exactly, but I like that he thinks that.

But then I start worrying. If he's just there to hide for a little while, that means he's planning to come home. But if he's just there for no reason then what's going to pull him back?

I know this is stupid.

I think this is stupid.

The news is playing the same footage, showing the same stills of the same places where the same people were shot.

They've started pulling over and searching every white van that drives by. That's insane. I'm glad we don't have a white van.

Mom says, "What is it, honey?"

I squirm. She doesn't use nicknames or pet names for me very often. But I guess she must know them, so maybe I should ask her how to spell Craiger. Craigor. Craiger. Oh, God, is this a metaphor? Or or or er er er.

I say, "Cody's school is having an open house. I talked to his mom and she says she'll drive me up to see him."

Mom studies me. "Really?"

I don't know why I would joke about this. "Yeah. I could stay overnight in the guest dorms—they have guest dorms or something, Mrs. Carter said—and then come home on Sunday."

Mom says, "Craig. I know you miss Cody, but do you really think going to visit him is the best idea?"

"He's not going to hurt me or anything."

"But, Craig, you had something special with him. And I know that . . . when he had to go away, it was a very hard time for you. You seem so happy now that you've made a new friend. I don't want you to get bogged down in those old feelings."

I don't know how she could figure all that out without realizing how bogged down I still am in those old feelings.

So I say, "Maybe I could get closure, Mom."

"Does Lio know about this?"

I shake my head.

She pauses, because she's waiting for me to say that I'll ask him before I go.

I don't say anything.

She says, "You'll miss karate if you're gone this weekend."

"I really don't care."

She glances at the TV. "Where's this school?"

"Pennsylvania."

"Ugh. Maybe it would be nice to get you out of town for a few days."

Lio—

I had the sudden urge to call you Liodore. Either I'm a freak who spends too much time on IM or all that talk about DEAD BROTHER (am I allowed to use the caps? Are those reserved to you?) got to my head.

I hope you're having a good time. You should go to one of New York's thriving gay clubs. Or something. Don't kiss any hot men. Though I doubt you could reach them. Maybe on your tiptoes. Do you dance on your tiptoes? Could you? It sounds amazing.

Craiger

C—

I'll be there.

Love,
Craigor

I really am not planning to do anything with Cody. I'm not, and still it feels like I'm cheating on Lio. On the drive up to Pennsylvania, Paul Simon on the radio, Cody's mom singing softly along while she twists her wedding ring, I feel like I'm cheating. Does motivation matter for cheating? Because this has nothing to do with Lio. I love Lio. But I love Cody, too.

And a few days ago, that was okay with me and okay with Lio, but a few days ago, I wasn't on my way to Cody's school. And I'm not so dumb that I don't know this changes things.

I say, "Am I old enough to fall in love?" Didn't Lio ask me this same question?

Mrs. Carter looks at me. "Oh, honey, you're old enough as soon as you realize there are other people in the world."

And she means this as a reassurance, I know it, and I can tell by her hand on the back of my neck, but, oh, God. I don't know if I'm there. I don't know. I don't know.

And she's only telling me that because I guess she still thinks Cody and I are together.

And Lio and I never officially got together. And Cody and I never officially broke up.

Christ.

It's just like Cody said. My heart is alive my heart is alive my heart is alive. I have Lio's heart. Fuck. What am I going to do with it?

What's love when you're too fucked up to feel it right?

I think it's a weapon.

Mrs. Carter says, "I wonder what these times do to you boys. I wonder so much."

We wait in the lobby while the lady at the desk calls Cody's room. This place looks like a hospital or a condominium.

I bounce from foot to foot.

And the doors to the elevator open and there he is. His hair's a little longer, his clothes a little less wrinkled, his eyes a little more tired than I've ever seen. I remind myself he's on medication, and maybe he's not himself. Maybe he's a lot different now.

Maybe he has a new boyfriend.

And he whispers, "Craig," and he ignores his mom and runs to me and pulls me in and hugs me so tightly.

He smells like Cody. Oh, my God, I missed him so much. He smells like home and like my heart and I want my heart back but I can't bear to take it from him because I think that he needs it and I think I am so warm in his arms right this second, and I hold my breath and I force myself to stop feeling like a murderer.

LIO

FIVE DAYS IN MOM'S APARTMENT IS ENOUGH TO
convince Michelle that she never wants to leave, and enough
to convince me that I'd be completely fine with never seeing
New York or my mother again. There's nothing like an old
home to show you how everything has changed.

Adelle roped me into doing a phone thing on Wednesday.
I ask her why we never talk about the day my mom left.
She asks if it's something I need to talk about.

Then I tell her about the day my mom left. I cry a little.
Then I go into the kitchen for dinner, and Michelle is
wearing a pair of Mom's earrings.

See, it's things like that.

I IM Jack and tell him I'm feeling crappy, and he tells me exactly the same thing Craig did, though I think Craig was joking: **go out have fun get wasted**

All right. Fine.

"I'm going out," I tell Michelle. She's making hot chocolate at the stove, which is so domestic it makes me want to puke.

"Where?"

"Just out."

"Be back by midnight."

What the fuck? "I'm going out!" I call to Mom, and I slam the door before I hear her answer. That's more than she did for us.

God, why am I here?

I meet up with some old friends of mine—Shawn and Tino, two turbo-gays I've known since seventh grade—and we meet in the park close to Vivo, this new club they insist drives Posh straight into the ground. Shawn has half a bottle of Jack Daniel's he stole from his father, and I take a small swallow every time it comes my way, which is many, many, many times. It tastes like the time my Mom sprayed Lysol on my sandwich when she was cleaning. Minus the sandwich. After a while, my mouth gets numb enough that I don't care.

My phone buzzes. I answer. It's Craig.

"Hey, baby," I say. "It's kinda late but I still miss youuuuu."

Shawn and Tino find two sticks and start pretending they're Luke and Darth Vader. I can't figure out which one is which.

He says, "Lio." His voice is really quiet. Is he crying? That's so sad. I don't want him to cry when I'm not there. "I need to talk to you."

"'Kay. Shoot."

"I'm with Cody right now."

Before my mouth was on fire from the Jack Daniel's, and now it feels like I'm chewing ice. "What?"

"I'm at his school. He's having an open house and I came to see him."

"Why . . . why did you do that?"

"I don't know. He's in the bathroom right now, and I just need to . . ."

"He's changed. *Tell me that.* It's been so long. He's gone and away and now you're with me."

"I'm with you. Listen to me, Lio, I'm with you. I'm just . . . I'm confused, and I didn't think it was fair not to tell you, and he hasn't changed, and I don't know if I've changed either."

I feel my heart rising up my chest. "*I've* changed! That's not fair! *I've changed!* I'm *talking* to you! You can't *tell me nothing's changed when here I am talking to you!* Why didn't you tell me you were going to see him?"

"Lio. Calm down."

"Listen to me! I'm talking *to you!"*

Shawn and Tino are all, "Whoa, listen to Lio all noisy."

"You're drunk." Craig's voice is hard. "This doesn't exactly count as you being really brave or something."

"Oh, GO FUCK YOUR BOYFRIEND!" I slam the two halves of my phone together.

He left. He's with Cody. I went away to New York for a few fucking days, and he goes back too. To his New York. I'm not making sense. But none of this is okay. I can't ever go back to where I was. I can't freak out and regress. I can't do that because there is no going back for me. I can't use the shit that's happened to me as an excuse to pretend I don't have a boyfriend who gets hurt when I freak out, because I didn't have anything when I didn't have a boyfriend. I had this city and this city will never be the same and it's not because of September 11th and it's not because of the sniper, it's because of Dad and Jasper and Craig and Craig's parents and his goddamn brother and Jack and *home*.

I'm here and the towers are gone and the people are dead and there's Craig, and he doesn't give a fuck, and no one he's given a shit about has ever died, Christ, the boy has five grandparents because one of them got divorced and remarried, and what the fuck does he know about anything, and he and Cody should probably just get together and make out because Jesus they're both going to be around forever so what's even the fucking point of cancer boys like me cancer boy cancer boy cancer boy.

"Give." I hold out my hand. I keep it out until Tino gives me the bottle, and I drink and drink and drink until Shawn pulls my arm away.

"Stop," he says, and he hits me on the back because I guess I'm coughing. There's Jack Daniel's coming out my nose.

"I want to dance," I say.

Shawn knows a guy who knows a guy who blew a guy and we're in the club no problem. I chain-smoke until my lungs threaten to catch fire. We have *X*s on our hands so we can't buy drinks. Big deal. We don't even have any money. And we're already drunk. Who gives a shit? No one I know.

"Have you heard about the shooting guy?" I ask this boy who's dancing with me. He's tall and looks like Craig. Here I go looking for Craig in everyone. This is the beginning of the end. Kiss me kiss me kiss me. He is not a boy. He is at least twenty-five and I like every year of him.

He says, "What?"

"They're calling him the betro sniper," I say. "No. Betro's not a word. Beltway sniper. Not metro. Beltway sniper."

"I don't know what you're talking about." He kisses me.

Someone somewhere is dying right now!

But it isn't me.

Statistically . . . ugh fuck that I thought I was over that shit.

Statistically, it could be me at any minute.

"Whoa." I push back from the boy. I'm going to fall over, but he catches me. I thought I was closer to the floor than this. Where are Shawn and Tino? "Whoa."

"You're all right, kid."

The music thrums at my ears and it feels like an attack, and I don't want it to stop. I feel it and I know it and I anticipate every beat before it happens. This is what my fight song is for. For fending off attackers. I am tough for a reason and it is to fucking destroy the music. I dance hard.

I don't know this song, but I know exactly what is happening right now. I know exactly what is . . . where are Shawn and Tino?

I put my forehead against this guy's chest. "Donttouch."

He says, "What's up with your hair, huh? You look like a little baby freak."

"I have cancer." I stand up and rub my eyes hard. "I'm from Washington, D.C. No, no, I'm not. I'm from Wheaton, Maryland!"

He gives me this small laugh. Is he as uncomfortable as I am? Craiger. "That's cool."

"And I have to go home," I say. "I should take the *train*. I don't want to fly by myself. Y'know what? They need to leave my city alone. Ima tell them. LEAVE MY CITY ALONE!"

The boy wraps his arms all the way around me and we're dancing, twirling around, spinning spinning spinning. He is warm and smells like deodorant. My cheek is wet but I don't think I'm crying. I think it's his sweat.

He says, "You are soooooo drunk, kid."

"I'm a virgin."

He says, "Oh . . ."

"Fuck me." I push my forehead into his chest. "Fuck me fuck me fuck me, I don't want to die a virgin. It's not fair. It's not fair not fair, don't let me die a virgin. I could drop dead at *any moment*."

He says, "All right, kid, it's time for you to try someone different. You're not coming home with me tonight. Too young."

"I'm not too . . ." I grab on to him. *"Take me home with you!"*

"Off, kid."

But I don't let go.

We've switched to a different song. I know this one. I listened to it over IM one time when Craig sent me the link and I said, **Im dancing around like a drag queen,** and he said, **so am I.**

"Dance with me," I say. I would whisper it but he would never hear me. It doesn't matter. He's never going to hear me there's so much news—noise, I meant to think noise— and this is a room full of other boys and I'm too small, no one's ever going to see me. *"I'm small because I have cancer!"* I scream.

He pushes me off. "Kid, cut it out, that's not funny."

He pushed me too hard. I'm on the floor. He doesn't offer his hand. He's gone. I've hit the ground hard and it hurts. Someone kicks me and it hurts. Did I hit my head? My stomach hurts. I'm not small enough because I haven't disappeared. Where are Shawn and Tino? Who cares, neither of them looks like Craig.

CRAIG

CODY WANTS TO SHOW ME EVERYTHING HE'S MADE
since he's been here, and it's more than I can believe,
canvas after sculpture after canvas. Some of the pills he's
taking must have switched on some artistic thing in his
brain. I know I'm bitter and angry and this is probably a
horrible thing to think, but it totally feels like every time
someone goes to any kind of rehabilitative place, whether
it's for drugs or abuse or attitude or whatever their problem
is, they all come out artists. Everyone's a fucking artist now.

And I want this to be evidence that Cody's changed
enough that I don't have to love him anymore. He wasn't
an artist when I loved him. So.

And then he turns to me with that big smile, that *I just won a soccer game* smile, the second his mom leaves the room, and he's going, "I missed you, I missed you, I missed you," and his voice is so soft and beautiful and exactly what I remembered, and there's his hand on my knee, and it feels like his hand and it feels like my knee, and even though we're in this awkward dorm that looks like a hospital room, I'm with the same boy who's been in my room, my room, my room, my bed.

"I missed you too," I whisper, because I did, and because I'm really not sure I believe in falling out of love, and because Lio was so mean and so drunk.

And now Cody is kissing me.

Shit, he's kissing me.

His hand is on my cheek, his fingers just centimeters away from my earlobe, and his other hand is in his lap, curled into the loosest fist.

His eyes are closed.

I pull back a little. "Cody . . ."

He watches me.

"I missed you," he says.

I nod a little.

He scrapes his finger against the edge of his desk, drawing up splinters of wood underneath his fingernail. I don't want to watch but I do anyway because it looks like it hurts.

He says, "I always had this fantasy that you'd just show up one day. I used to imagine it. I'd be sitting in class or therapy or something, and you'd appear in the doorway, here to rescue me."

I nod a little.

I should tell him to stop scratching his desk.

"I missed you," he says again.

"I missed you too," I whisper.

And I missed his hands and his hair and . . . everything about him is the boy I poured into me, the boy I wanted more than I'd ever wanted anything.

He says, "I always kind of hoped you were waiting, like those wives when their husbands go off to war. That's so stupid."

"I was waiting."

"Then who's the guy?" he says, in the back of his throat.

I don't know what to do, so I just say, "He's Lio."

"Then what the fuck happened to waiting?"

The fact that I am afraid he is going to hit me right now should tell me everything I need to know. It doesn't. But I can close my eyes and see Lio, so angry so drunk and so stable and so right now. And so willing to listen.

"I stopped," is all I can say, because it is the only truth.

There's no reason. It's just what happened. I stopped waiting because that was the part of the story that came next for me.

He looks so heartbroken, and I don't know what to do.

"I'm sorry," I whisper. But sorry is all I can be for him right now.

I'm not even doing this for Lio, but for me.

And it sucks.

Cody has to sleep a lot, but he says it's okay, I can stay, he won't wake up. He's a heavy sleeper now. He never used to be.

But he did always sleep, so much. Whenever he was upset, he'd sleep. It was like crying or something.

Until he stopped sleeping and stopped crying. At least I still do one of the two. So does Lio.

I call him. It's two in the morning, and I'm supposed to be in the guest dorms. I shouldn't be in this room. I promised the night nurse that I was leaving any minute. I shouldn't have left Maryland. It doesn't feel right not to be there now.

Lio shouldn't pick up. He should be asleep. He should be too scared to talk on the phone even if he is awake, because he's Lio, and he can't have gotten better all by himself, he can't have fixed himself.

And then I hear rustling around and his phone click on.

He fixed himself.

"Hello?" His voice is so tiny and crackly.

Everything I wanted to say to him is gone. I don't even

know what it was, because right now all I know is Lio needs me. He needs me. I can feel it. It's somewhere in my stomach.

Cody's crying in his sleep. Shit.

"What's going on?" I ask Lio, quietly. "What's wrong?"

"'M throwing up."

"Ohhhh." My stomach really does hurt. "Oh. You drank too much."

"Drank. Too. Much."

"Where are you?"

"The bathroom. The flooooooor."

"At home?"

"Mom's."

"That's what I meant, yeah."

I listen to him throw up for a minute. God. He sounds like he's about to bring up his pancreas.

"Breathe," I tell him, when I hear him come back to the phone. "Poor thing. Breathe."

"'M so good at throwing up, put it on a resume."

It's hard not to roll my eyes at him sometimes, I swear. "Poor little cancerboy."

"Kissed someone."

"Yeah?" I sigh. "I'm not really surprised."

"Was stupid. All of it so stupid. Did you kiss Cody?"

"He kissed me. Didn't kiss back."

He exhales. "I suck."

Oh. "No, it's okay. I . . . I kind of like screwing up a little less than you. For once." Because I'm not angry either.

Because it's not as if he started this. This whole time, he has been the one reaching out, offering out that shattered heart to me with both hands, like in that ring he wears. And I kicked my feet against the ground and went I don't knooooooooow, Lio, I don't knooooow, and what was I expecting to happen? Did I think he'd wait?

But he did. I don't ever want to give him a reason to stop.

My stomach feels warm all of a sudden.

He waited for me.

He says, "I called your brother."

"What?"

"I was sad and I called your brother."

"You're not going to kill yourself. Don't say that."

"It's his day off. I called him at your house."

I breathe. "What did he say?"

"He said, *Don't kill yourself, Lio.*"

"Don't do it."

"I'm not gonna. I promised. You know what, Craig? This is love in the time of shit," he says, and then he's throwing up again.

"Yeah," I say. "But love love love love love love."

I kneel next to Cody and wipe the tears off his cheeks. "Don't cry," I whisper to him. "I will always love you. I promise."

Because I can give him that, but I can never get back to the place where it will mean anything to him. I kiss his cheek to close the door.

Once I'm in the guest dorms, the internet finally decides to tell me, at 3 a.m., that a man was shot six hours ago in Ashland, Virginia.

He was in a parking lot outside a restaurant.

It couldn't have been me or Lio or Cody, because we're all out of town. And none of us would have been in Virginia, anyway. It really couldn't have been Lio, logically. It could not have been Lio.

But

it could have been Lio.

And I can't get that thought out of my brain no matter what I do. It could have been Lio. We fought and we hung up and *what if it had been Lio?*

I still don't believe it could have been me. I don't know if I ever will. I don't know if that stupid heartbeat in my head is ever going to shut up enough for me to realize that I'm human even though I am some big bad invincible teenager me me me. But Lio, Lio is human, Lio is a stupid imperfect human with stupid hair who gets drunk and stupid like a heart-aching fifteen-year-old and *it could have been him* and that is enough reason to be concerned.

This guy who was shot was thirty-seven, but twenty-two years ago he might have been someone's Lio.

It could have been Lio.

There could have been a sniper in New York tonight.

He could have gotten alcohol poisoning.

He could have choked on a wine cork.

He could have gotten cancer.

It could have been Lio. It could have been Lio Lio Lio Lio Lio.

Nothing else matters. And all of it matters, because everything is in the same world as him. Everyone in the whole world is in this room with him.

But tonight it's all about him, and the whole world is an incubator to make Lio the best man he can be, and I want to help, and I want to be a hand on him, a good hand, and I want everything in this whole world to take care of him. And I am going to help.

Though, the truth is, that kid can take care of himself, and I'm sorry but that is the most spectacular fucking thing I can ever remember.

I think about Cody, and this isn't really a decision, not really. The truth is that it never was.

And this all would have been easier if Cody had changed, or if Cody were still truly unavailable and not just inconvenient, or if there were some tangible, understandable reason we couldn't be together. There isn't. And the bottom line is, there isn't any ending here, not really. He hugs me good-bye, and I can tell he wants to kiss me, and I want to kiss him, too, but I hold up my hand and shake my head.

There's nothing movie-script ending about this, and I still love him, and in the car I think *what if what if.* I don't know if I'll ever get closure, the way Lio says he did when his brother died. It still sucks that we're not together, and a part of my life will probably always suck because it's not happening with Cody, but I'm going home, and I'm going home to Lio.

And he comes straight to my house from the airport, and he runs through my door in that zigzag and I shout, "Run, Lio, run," and I kiss him in my kitchen like I've never kissed anyone in my life. It feels a little hilarious, like I'm trying to sweep his whole body into mine. Starting with hands, then arms, then lips.

Then I take his head between both my hands and say, "Are you okay?"

He isn't pale or scared or throwing up. He's looking up at me with that smile that could wake the dead. "I'm awe-some." He yanks my head down and kisses me hard.

Yeah. He's awesome.

"Do you want to talk about seeing Cody?" he asks me. "Must have been hard."

I shake my head. "I don't have anything new to say about him. Want to talk about your Mom?"

"I'm not okay with her."

I nod a little.

"I hate talking."

I give him a half smile. I hope I look sympathetic.

He breathes out like I'm such a hard thing to put up with, and then he says, "How about I tell you what color I want to paint my room?"

And there's that grin again.

After he tells me—dark green—we talk some more and we figure out that what we really want to talk about is how we want to spend every possible minute together until our parents make us go back to school.

Because we're fifteen and kind of stupid, and this is how we do love.

And I know I've said enough sappy shit, but this is kind of the way I always wanted to do it.

And when this is all over, and we have to go back to school and come out of my basement and be in the real world and deal with all of the real-world shit,

when all of this trickles

and

stops

I am going to help Lio paint his room.

L10

"SO ARE YOU STILL ANGRY?" ADELLE ASKS ME.

I say, "Not all the time. But mostly, yeah. I'm still pissed off that my mom turned out to be just as much of a use-less . . . just as useless as I thought she was. And I wish my dad had more time for me, even though I know he's trying. And I'm pissed Michelle's probably going to end up going back to New York for good. And I'm mad Craig still loves Cody."

She says, "Okay. And in a larger sense?"

"Larger?"

"Less immediate."

"I guess I wish Cody's dad hadn't died in September

eleventh, even though Craig and I probably wouldn't be together right now if he hadn't. And . . ." I shrug. "I'm still really pissed that my brother died and left us with all this love to figure out how to shift around without him here."

Adelle studies me. "So what are you going to do?"

"I don't know. I'll probably always be pissed off about all this. It's not like everything's suddenly perfect. People are still getting shot all over the place. And not even in Maryland alone. I only care about people in this area more because it's home."

"Proximity."

"Yeah." I shrug. "Fair enough."

"Go on." She's not as afraid of interrupting me anymore.

"I guess . . . it's hard to believe that things are suddenly going to be okay because people are still going to get shot as far into the future as I can see. And outside of the D.C. suburbs, probably everyone will have forgotten in a few years."

"But you'll remember."

"But maybe I'll have Craig. That's what's important to me right now."

"You're allowed to have a rough time, you know." She's writing on her pad. "You're allowed to express that you're having a rough time too."

"I know. And I will. But maybe not today. Craig's mom got me ice cream on the way here. I'm sorry, I'm probably way too happy to be worth your time."

She laughs a little.

But I don't need her to tell me that I'll be sad again. There will be days I wake up sweating and crying because I dreamed about Theodore and he's not here, and I'm the only person in the world who looks like me. Craig is still emailing Cody, and there will probably be days that really gets under my skin. Right now, I can't give a shit. I'm the one in Craig's house. I'm the one he whispers about before he goes to sleep.

I tell her, "I'm basically made of perspective right now."

She's still smiling. "What are your plans for this week?"

"See you. Besides that, hide? Run when I'm outside? Duck if I see a white van? I have to go back to school, which sucks, but I'm basically living at Craig's house. My dad's letting me. Apparently, he knew I was gay the whole time." We found Craig's last cat yesterday. She'd had kittens, which seems too perfect to even be real. I say, "I'm auditioning for the GSA talent show—because my friend Jack is *making* me—and Craig says we're doing some sort of protest today. Which . . . I'm terrified about."

She raises her eyebrows. "Outside?"

"I know. He hasn't told me any details. But he won't let me get hurt."

She says, "Craig can't protect you from everything."

I look down and nod and say, "I know."

And that's okay.

Craig and his mom pick me up from therapy, and I check my messages on my cell phone. Dad called and said he loves me and misses me. I'll call him back later. I know he's worried and probably would rather I was home, but I'm too comfortable here right now.

Here's the protest, it turns out. Craig and I lie on our stomachs in the basement with the animals, two sheets of poster board, and a lot of paint. We groan when the animals walk through the paint, and my poster ends up with kitten footprints all over it. Craig dabs paint on my nose, which devolves into sneezing and tickling and kissing.

It takes us way too long to finish our posters, with all our screwing around, but eventually we're done. Mine says PEACE and Craig's says LOVE.

We stand out in his backyard, in the open air, in this random-as-fuck suburb, with our posters in the air and our fingers laced and our faces up to the sky. No one will ever see us.

Safe, I whisper, like we're sliding into home.

Then Craig grabs my hand as we go inside and says, "And now for the real protest."

"What?"

He pulls me into his bathroom and digs through the cabinet under the sink. Then he sits me down on the floor and leans my head back into the bathtub. I figure out then exactly what he's doing, and I think about stopping him, but I don't. Instead, I talk him through it. I'm kind of an expert at this by now.

Two hours later, I'm blond again.

I touch my reflection and Craig kisses my cheek.

"No hat," he says.

I nod.

He drops his voice like he doesn't want anyone to hear him. "I can see you."

And I damn near swallow him whole.

CRAIG

OUR FIRST DAY BACK AT SCHOOL, TODD SUBS FOR A second-period class. Right after, he meets me at my locker and says, "Is today important?"

I don't know how to answer this question.

He says, "I mean, if I pulled you out of school right now, would it be a major detriment to the health of your education?"

I've barely been to school this month, so it's not like I'm really on track to being an upstanding citizen anyway. "Let's go."

"I'll pull the car around. Stay inside."

✗ ✗ ✗

I leave a note on Lio's locker. *Spending the day with my brother. BREAK A LEG!!!!*

His audition for the talent show is today. I wanted to go see him, but, to be honest, I've heard him sing, and I'm not sure the GSA is really my scene. Maybe someday. I do love community. I'll be at the show, anyway, and right now, I really want to be with my brother, wherever he wants to take me.

Fishing, it turns out.

He hands me a floppy hat and takes me to fucking West Virginia for the afternoon. He says he's never felt safer in his life. I throw all my fish back, and he throws his back too, just to humor me.

He tells me a shitload of dirty jokes that I have to remember to tell Lio. He gathers me under his arm and tells me the point of working nights was supposed to be so he had days free. And he's going to work on it. We talk about Lio, and about this girl at work who he thinks maybe, maybe . . .

He has no obligation to me. He's not my parent. He's just my big brother. And this is just one of the best days of my life.

LIO

THE AUDITION IS PRETTY MUCH A JOKE, BECAUSE everyone who auditions for the talent show gets in. I mean, it's the GSA. But the audition decides the order of the program. You really want to be toward the beginning or the end, Jack explains to me. We're in the back of the auditorium, watching a girl tap dance.

He says, "They put the second best act at the beginning and the very best at the end. In the middle is pure shit."

"I'm scared," I say.

"Oh, shut up. You're going to be awesome."

"You've never heard me sing. I could be horrible."

"You certainly give your voice plenty of rest." He smiles at me.

It's true, I'm still pretty quiet, even though I talk a lot more than I used to, especially to Jack and Craig. But I'm never going to be a chatterbox like them.

"I'm going to cheer for you when you're done," Jack says. "Like, really loudly and obnoxiously. I might actually stand up and do that really loud clap, with cupped hands? Purely to piss you off."

"I might kill you."

"Yeah, I know."

"I might . . . castrate you or bring you to a gay bar."

"I've experienced one of those already. You can probably figure out which one."

"Hmm . . ."

He still has me in a headlock when the head auditioner, the sparkliest, shiniest boy imaginable, says, "Lio?"

Jack releases me and gives me a high five. Break a leg.

He smiles at me the whole time I'm onstage. I sing the best I can. I don't forget the words. The sparkly boy smiles and thanks me. Jack jumps to his feet and cheers, and I love every minute of it.

I get the first spot in the program. Not too shabby. Plus, it's fucking first.

CRAIG

I'VE FOUND ALL THE ANIMALS EXCEPT FOR ONE.
My guinea pig, Peggy.

I will still go out looking, and I'll still wait for calls from
the shelter, but I am not going to make it my whole world.
I can't. I have too many animals and too many things in my
life to pour all of me into a lost guinea pig. I will imagine
her in a warm new home with new owners. I will worry
about her sometimes.

I will let her go.

It's like a voice in my head has said, *enough*. Or, as Lio
would say, "Let it be."

Maybe the voice in my head is Lio.

Tuesday morning, before school, I tell all of this to Dad in this voice that doesn't sound nearly as hopeful as I would like it to. Dad tells me Todd would tell me not to kill myself, and he takes me out for pancakes before Lio wakes up.

"I feel so bad," I tell him. "I should have been looking out for them better. I was pretty much a pretty shitty . . . whatever I was to them, I was pretty shitty about it."

He says, really softly, "Craig."

"Peggy should have been in a cage."

"You had a cage for her?"

I nod. "She should have been in it. I should have put her in."

"Craig," Dad says. And he takes a deep breath. "You had to let her out of the cage. I . . . kid, in a way, I'm glad this goddamn break-in happened."

My chin shakes. "Why?"

He puts my hand on my shoulder. "To let you out of your cage."

So that's it, really. I will need to deal with this. I'll still miss Peggy all the time, but I need to keep going where I'm going.

So here is what I have.

Four dogs.

Eight cats (but I think I am going to give the kittens away).

Two rabbits.

One mouse.

A koala.

I get out of the car to feed the animals who are here to be fed and Dad turns on the news. I hear Lio's alarm go off upstairs. His alarm is so loud because that boy can sleep through anything. He says it's a consequence of growing up with six girls.

A bus driver was shot, fifteen minutes ago. Close to here again. Standing on the steps of his bus. And the news decides this is the time to read a bit of the note that the sniper left on Saturday. *Do not release to the press,* it says and here they are, releasing it to us. This feels like the worst idea in the world. The note says:

Your children are not safe, anywhere, at any time.

My breathing hurts.

I say, "I'm not going to school today," as Lio trudges down the stairs, rubbing his eyes. Mine feel like they're catching fire. I don't like this. I don't like this and I really don't like that note.

Dad is watching me and he says, "Okay."

"What's going on?" Mom says. She's coming down the stairs behind Lio. She kisses the top of his head, and he gives her a sleepy smile before he turns his focus to the news.

He takes a second to process what's going on, then he puts his hand on my shoulder.

"I'm scared," I say. I blurt it out. Here it is. I don't know why I'm scared *now*, surrounded by walls, with my parents and Lio right here. But I am. This should be the place where I'm safe. This should be it.

He gives me one of those small smiles he used to give me back when he didn't talk. His eyes are so close to me that for a minute I think I'm looking in a mirror, even though his eyes are blue and I know mine aren't. I realize how scary it would be if Theodore was still around. And how amazing. And I feel for a minute like I'm going to cry, but it passes, because Lio's still looking at me.

He whispers, "Want to hear a secret?"

I nod.

"You're safe with me anywhere, at all times."

It turns out, our "anywhere" is the basement, and our "at all times" is the entire day. We don't go to school. We play checkers and make out. My parents are upstairs watching the news. And even though it feels like the entire world is freaking out, and even though the entire world is really just our area, and no one else anywhere gives a shit, and they definitely don't give a shit that there are two boys making out in a basement, that's what we are, we keep doing it, and there is something sort of beautiful about the fact that we keep doing that even now that we know it's not what the world is about.

If I could take all the machine guns in the world and bend them into hearts, I totally totally would, even if I got grazed by bullets in the process, which knowing me I probably would, because I'm a little bit of a klutz, but Lio thinks I'm cute.

LIO

THAT NIGHT I DECIDE, *ENOUGH DAWDLING.*

I get out of bed at two in the morning, which is difficult, because, despite the rubbery mattress, it is warm and lovely under the covers. And out of bed, it's freezing. It has become mid-autumn completely without my knowledge. Most of October is gone. It feels like we should get to try this month over. Not the things that happened, just the season. We didn't notice it getting cold.

I put on a pair of socks, consider my feet, and put on another pair of socks. I don't want to get sick.

Todd is already at work, and Craig's parents are sleeping. Across town, my family is asleep, except my mother in New York, who is drinking or sleeping, and my grown-up sisters, who are probably just drinking. I think when we sleep, the world belongs to everyone still awake. Which means a whole shitload of the world belongs to Craig.

I whisper his name from the top of the stairs.

He rolls over in his bed and looks at me. He isn't emailing. He's lying there.

"Come upstairs," I tell him.

He moans a little. "God, my parents . . ."

"Like this is about your parents." I know what that room is to him. "Come on. I'm sick of looking at all your stupid trophies and drawings all by myself. Come tell me what they mean."

He wraps his arms around himself. "The animals . . ."

"Can come up or stay down here," I say.

He watches me. I lean my cheek against the banister.

"Pleeeeease, Craig?"

He gets out of bed, shivering, and says, "Come here."

"Why?"

"Cold. Too hard to find a sweatshirt." He grabs me by the legs and lifts me onto his back. I like this. I kick my feet all the way upstairs. I hope I'm keeping him warm.

It's Tuesday night, and we've been together for three months or three days or something, and it's been the best time of my life.

And let's be honest, I have no idea how many three days or three months I have left.

"I really like you," I tell him.

He drops me on the rubbery mattress and kisses me.

"You know that kid who got shot?" I say. "Outside Michelle's school?"

He's breathing hard between kisses. "Uh-huh?"

"He's totally going to be fine. Saw it on the news."

We are in the bed, squeaking on the mattress. We are all arms and legs and mouths. I've never kissed like this before. I feel like I'm falling into him.

"I like your hair," he says.

"Mmm."

His hand underneath my T-shirt. I shiver. "However far you want to go, Craig."

"Yeah?"

"It's fine with me. I'm ready."

He kisses me hard, for a long time. His teeth are against my lips.

He whispers, "Li? Can we just sleep tonight?"

I can't say I'm not a little disappointed. But it's all right. There *will* be other nights. There will be. I have to believe that. And again and again and again.

I wrap my arms as far around him as they will go. "We can sleep forever. I promise I won't go crazy."

"Don't get cancer."

"I won't. Don't, um, get a dog."

He chuckles, and we kiss. And he falls asleep with his lips against mine.

He sleeps. My fucking boyfriend is asleep, and maybe tomorrow he'll wake up without that headache or that bleary look in his eyes or the ringing in his ears from staying up for thirty hours. He sleeps so close to me, like he's doing it just to prove to me that he'll be okay.

It is so much more beautiful than any polar bears in Alaska. Because I am here and he is mine and forever is as long as we want it to be.

The rest, as they say, is history.

Like a lot of mornings, we wake up and there is news. They've arrested two men at a rest stop. The sniper rifles were in their trunk of their car. A man found them. They were asleep.

ACKNOWLEDGMENTS

THIS BOOK COULD NOT HAVE EXISTED WITHOUT the support of my amazing editor, Anica Rissi, or my agent, Suzie Townsend. I cannot emphasize enough how much of a role these two had in shaping the final draft of this book. Suzie always knows where I need to add words, and Anica always knows where I need to cross them out. Without the two of them, I would never know what my books were about. They're invaluable. Thank you as well to everyone else at Simon Pulse and FinePrint Literary. It's an honor to be working with you.

My best friend, Alex Stek, read *Gone, Gone, Gone* a page at a time while I was writing the first draft. He pretended it was perfect.

My family, on the other hand, deserves a million thank-yous for putting up with the fact that I don't let them read my books until they're on the shelves. My mother, my father, and my sister are three of the best people I have ever met, and they prove it every day by somehow tolerating me. Thank you as well to Seth, Emma, Galen, and my cousins, who are all family as well, some more obviously than others.

I don't know how to address the people who were affected by the 2002 Beltway Sniper attacks except to say that I hope this story reaches you if you want it and doesn't if you don't.

I'm useless without the Musers, and almost as useless without my magic gay fish.

And I owe a million thank-yous, as always, to you. I do it for you, you know?

ABOUT THE AUTHOR

HANNAH MOSKOWITZ is the author of *Break, Invincible Summer,* and the middle-grade novel *Zombie Tag*. She was in Maryland the whole time, and she has owned a total of fourteen pets. Visit her at untilhannah.com.

How far is too far?

Break

by Hannah Moskowitz

From
BREAK

THE FIRST FEELING IS EXHILARATION.

My arms hit the ground. The sound is like a mallet against a crab.

Pure fucking exhilaration.

Beside me, my skateboard is a stranded turtle on its back. The wheels shriek with each spin.

And then—oh. *Oh,* the pain.

The second feeling is pain.

Naomi's camera beeps and she makes a triumphant noise in her throat. "You *totally* got it that time," she says. "Tell me you got it."

I hold my breath for a moment until I can say, "We got it."

"You fell like a bag of mashed potatoes." Her sneakers make bubble gum smacks against the pavement on her way to me. "Just . . . splat."

So vivid, that girl.

Naomi's beside me, and her tiny hand is an ice cube on my smoldering back.

"Don't get up," she says.

I choke out a sweaty, clogged piece of laughter. "Wasn't going to, babe."

"Whoa, you're bleeding."

"Yeah, I thought so." Blood's the unfortunate side effect of a hard-core fall. I pick my head up and shake my neck, just to be sure I can. "This was a definitely a good one."

I let her roll me onto my back. My right hand stays pinned, tucked grotesquely under my arm, fingers facing back toward my elbow.

She nods. "Wrist's broken."

"Huh, you think?" I swallow. "Where's the blood?"

"Top of your forehead."

I sit up and lean against Naomi's popsicle stick of a body and wipe the blood off my forehead with my left hand. She gives me a quick squeeze around the shoulders, which is basically as affectionate as Naomi gets. She'd probably shake hands on her deathbed.

She takes off her baseball cap, brushes back her hair, and replaces the cap with the brim tilted down. "So what's the final tally, kid?"

Ow. Shit. "Hold on a second."

She waits while I pant, my head against my skinned knee. Colors explode in the back of my head. The pain's almost electric.

"Hurt a lot?" she asks.

I expand and burst in a thousand little balloons. "Remind me why I'm doing this again?"

"Shut up, you."

I manage to smile. "I know. Just kidding."

"So what hurts? Where's it coming from?"

"My brain."

She exhales, rolling her eyes. "And your brain is getting these pain signals from where, sensei?"

"Check my ankles." I raise my head and sit up, balancing on my good arm. I suck on a bloody finger and click off my helmet. The straps flap around my chin. I taste like copper and dirt.

I squint sideways into the green fluorescence of the 7-Eleven. No one inside has noticed us, but it's only a matter of time. Damn. "Hurry it up, Nom?"

She takes each of my sneakered feet by the toe and moves it carefully back and forth, side to side, up and down. I close my eyes and feel all the muscles, tendons, and bones shift perfectly.

"Anything?"

I shake my head. "They're fine."

"Just the wrist, then?"

"No. There's something else. It-it's too much pain to be just the wrist. . . . It's somewhere. . . ." I gesture weakly.

"You seriously can't tell?"

"Just give me a second."

Naomi never gets hurt. She doesn't understand. I think she's irritated until she does that nose-wrinkle. "Look, we're not talking spinal damage or something here, right? Because I'm going to feel really shitty about helping you in your little mission if you end up with spinal damage."

I kick her to demonstrate my un-paralysis.

She smiles. "Smart-ass."

I breathe in and my chest kicks. "Hey. I think it's the ribs."

Naomi pulls up my T-shirt and checks my chest. While she takes care of that, I wiggle all my fingers around, just to check. They're fine—untouched except for scrapes from the pavement. I dig a few rocks from underneath a nail.

"I'm guessing two broken ribs," she says.

"Two?"

"Yeah. Both on the right."

I nod, gulping against the third feeling—nausea.

"Jonah?"

I ignore her and struggle to distract myself. Add today to the total, and that's 2 femurs + 1 elbow + 1 collarbone + 1 foot + 4 fingers + 1 ankle + 2 toes + 1 kneecap + 1 fibula + 1 wrist + 2 ribs.

= 17 broken bones.

189 to go.

Naomi looks left to the 7-Eleven. "If we don't get out of here soon, someone's going to want to know if you're okay. And then we'll have to find another gross parking lot for next time."

"Relax. I'm not doing any more skateboard crashes."

"Oh, yeah?"

"Enough with the skateboard. We've got to be more creative next time, or your video's gonna get boring."

She makes that wicked smile. "You okay to stand?" She takes my good hand and pulls me up. My right wrist dangles off to the side like the limb of a broken marionette. I want to hold it up, but Naomi's got me in a death grip so I won't fall.

My stomach clenches. I gasp, and it kills. "Shit, Nom."

"You're okay."

"I'm gonna puke."

"Push through this. Come on. You're a big boy."

Any other time, I would tease her mercilessly for this comment. And she knows it. Damn this girl.

I'm upright, but that's about as far as I'm going to go. I lean against the grody wall of the Laundromat. "Just bring the car around. I can't walk that far."

She makes her hard-ass face. "There's nothing wrong with your legs. I'm not going to baby you."

My mouth tastes like cat litter. "Nom."

She shakes her hair and shoves down the brim of her cap. "You really do look like crap."

She always expects me to enjoy this part. She thinks a boy who likes breaking bones has to like the pain.

Yeah. Just like Indiana Jones loves those damn snakes.

I do begging eyes.

"All right," she says. "I'll get the car. Keep your ribs on."

This is Naomi's idea of funny.

She slouches off. I watch her blur into a lump of sweatshirt, baseball cap, and oversize jeans.

Shit. Feeling number four is worry. Problems carpet bomb my brain.

What am I going to tell my parents? How is this setting a good example for Jesse? What the hell am I doing in the grossest parking lot in the city on a Tuesday night?

The feeling that never comes is regret.

There's no room. Because you know you're three bones closer.

SOME GIRLS ARE ADDICTIVE.

INVINCIBLE SUMMER
BY HANNAH MOSKOWITZ

"ENGROSSING, MESSY, COMPLEX, AND REAL.
MOSKOWITZ'S WRITING IS RAW AND SO RIGHT."
—LAUREN STRASNICK, author of *Nothing Like You*

From
INVINCIBLE SUMMER

S he's eleven!" Noah and I protest the entire time Melinda's patting our sister's face with powder and dabbing lip gloss on her baby mouth. "Too young for makeup," I whine, and Noah drops his head onto Bella's pillow so he can't watch. But I can't look away. Bella and I are riveted— Bella by how old Claudia looks, me by the length of Melinda's fingers.

"I'm only giving her a little, Chasey." Melinda traces powder over the tops of Claudia's eyes. "Making her feel just as beautiful as she is."

Claudia's positively beaming.

"She's going to be swarmed," Noah says, his voice muffled. "Do you want her swarmed by *men*?"

Claudia laughs, all grown-up in the back of her throat. *Ha ha ha.*

"Maybe someone will fall in love with her," Bella says, and bites her lip and looks at me.

Noah looks at me, telling me it's my turn to object. "Too young to be someone's lust object," I say, then turn to Bella and mouth *Eleven*, to clarify. Bella had her makeup done before we got here, and now she's studying herself in the mirror, pinching her cheekbones and pressing the skin between her eyebrows.

"You're all too young to be talking about this love and lust shit," Noah says.

Melinda is calm, blowing extra eye shadow off her fingers. "The point is not to be loved. The point is to love." She puts on some kind of accent. "'*For there is merely bad luck in not being loved; there is misfortune in not loving.*'"

Noah picks up his head. "What's that?"

"Camus, darling." Melinda takes a book from the foot of her bunk and tosses it down to Noah. "Only the most summer-oriented philosopher in the book."

"What book?" says Bella.

Melinda examines her eyeliner pencil. "The book of life, my dear."

"Man," Claudia says. "That's one big book."

"Small font, too." Noah sits up and cracks open the paperback. "He's French?"

"*Oui*, but that's supposed to be the best translation." Melinda gathers her curly hair back in one hand and leans forward, examining Claudia's eyebrows. "You guys would like him."

Noah reads, "'*Turbulent childhood, adolescent daydreams in the drone of the bus's motor, mornings, unspoiled girls, beaches, young muscles always at the peak of their effort, evening's slight anxiety in a sixteen-year-old heart, lust for life, fame, and ever the same sky through the years, unfailing in strength and light, itself insatiable, consuming one by one over a period of months the victims stretched out in the form of crosses on the beach at the deathlike hour of noon.*'"

We're quiet.

"Well." Claudia flinches at the mascara wand. "That was happy."

"Shut up," Noah says. "I'd almost believe he grew up here."

I look at him, and I know by the way he's smiling that I'm making the same face I always make when we agree. The one that looks really shocked.

"I think it's beautiful," Bella says, quietly.

"*No love without a little innocence,*" Melinda recites, putting on that silly accent again.

Noah says, "Hmm," and sticks the paperback in his pocket. "All right. You kids ready to go?"

The Jolly Roger isn't much of an amusement park, and it's farther away than we'll usually stand to travel when we're down here, but every few years we all get it in our heads that we need to go. We grab Shannon and Gideon from the living room, stuff ourselves into the van, and we're off to see the creaky fun house and the carousel and the clumsy juggler.

All the windows are down and the wind sounds like someone yelling at us, but we're laughing so hard we barely hear it. The girls rake their fingers through their hair to keep the tangles out, but it's hopeless and they know it and it's okay. The lights on every restaurant, mini-golf-course, ice-cream stand, and motel rush by just like the people, who are all dressed ten times better than they ever are during the year and trying ten times less hard. I feel like we're stuck in a movie reel, roaring through as hard as we can and spinning the world into streaks.

"*Gods of summer they were at twenty,*" Melinda says.

It takes Noah a few minutes to find this quote in his book.

"'Gods of summer they were at twenty by their enthusiasm for life, and they still are, deprived of all hope. I have seen two of them die. They were full of horror, but silent.'"

Melinda takes her eyes off the road to examine us all in the rearview mirror. Claudia, for a minute, stops punching Gideon and looks at us, her artificially enlarged eyes artificially sparkling. She's beautiful—just normal, unscary beautiful—without all the makeup, but she never carries herself like she is.

"Which two?" Claudia asks.

Noah's glued back to the book. "It could be an exaggeration."

"I need to get a copy of this book," I say.

Noah nods. "You so do, Chase. And so do I. . . ."

"What's mine is yours," Melinda says softly. "As long as I eventually get it back."

We park and wait by the ticket booths, calculating how much money we have and how many rides we need to go on. I'm trying to track everyone with my eyes; I feel older than the twins but younger than Claudia, who's standing with Melinda, tossing her matted hair, while Bella and Shannon shriek and climb on each other's backs. Gideon falls down. "Everyone needs tickets," I say. "Someone has to watch—"

"I've got it." Noah gives me one of those rare, reassuring

smiles. "Melinda and I will take Gideon, okay? And you stay with Claude and the twins."

I yank Gideon off the ground and sign **Noah stay.**

Noah run Gideon says, and I try not to concentrate on that.

Stay me? Noah signs.

I realize that we never try to do anything to Gideon without asking his permission. Even though he's six, and I don't think considering a six-year-old's opinion usually comes with the territory. Some parts of being deaf are pretty sweet, I guess.

Gid spins around for a little while, then falls down again and signs **OK.**

"C'mere, you." Noah hauls Gideon onto his back and smiles at Melinda. "We've got him."

This finally hits me. "Yeah, and what are you going to do with Gideon while you're with Melinda?"

"Cover his eyes."

"Oh, ha ha," I call to their backs.

Claudia and Shannon want to ride the log flume, so we walk across the park, crunching the gravel beneath our sandals. Every few steps Bella will look at me and smile. Whenever a girl from school is nice to me like this, I'm always tripping over myself figuring out how far I'm going to try to get with her and freezing up before I can do anything. But here, I have this feeling that I can't screw this up, and there's no point in planning anything, because what's going to happen is going to happen. It's as predictable as the carousel.

She doesn't want to get splashed, so we stand under the pavilion while Shannon and Claude get in line. Bella's wearing a pink skirt, and the breeze sometimes hitches it above her knees. Her legs are starting to tan, or maybe it's that brown lotion girls use to pretend. Either way, I like it even more than I would have expected.

"Really nice night, isn't it?" she says.

"Mmm-hmm."

She revolves, looking at the lights from the Ferris wheel bouncing off the water for the paddleboats. "I love it here."

"I love everywhere here." I rub the back of my neck. "I seriously wish we could live here, even in the off-season. Like, even when it's cold, this has got to be good."

"We come down in the fall and winter sometimes. I almost like it better. No people around, everything so gray . . . It feels really old. Like you're looking at this town a hundred years ago."

"When our forefathers ran around barefoot."

She smiles at me. "Exactly."

There's no one else under the pavilion, and with the

amusement park bouncing off Bella's eyes and the dusty pink of her skirt, I can almost pretend we are a hundred years old and we know everything. When, really, the only thing I know is that I'm going to kiss her, but I'm not going to try anything more. And she's smiling because she knows it too.

It's not really that we're old so much as we've existed forever. We're in a black-and-white photo. The only color comes from the Ferris wheel lights and her skirt.

We're eternalized in the film. Forever kids. We are our forefathers today.

I kiss her, and her mouth tastes like wax and peppermint.

It's not my first kiss, but it *feels* like it. Like I'm watching a movie of my first.

She pulls back, laughing. "Chase, you bit my lip."

Or a blooper reel. "I did? Sorry."

She giggles and turns, and I smell the powder on her cheek. I want to kiss her. I want to bake cookies with her. I want to watch her put on her makeup like I got to watch Claudia.

"Look." She points to the top of the flume. "They're going down."

"Shannon looks *terrified*."

"He's just hoping Claudia will hold his hand."

We watch Claudia and Shannon take the plunge, and I wrap my fingers around Bella's palm.

"Chase."

I look up from Camus. "Shh shh shh." I jerk my head to Noah, crashed on top of his covers, shoes still on. "He's asleep. And still, for once." Noah's always waking me up by thrashing around when he's sleeping. It's the worst.

Claudia tilts from one foot to the other, doing the same little dance that Gideon does. I close the paperback and say, "You're supposed to be asleep, beautiful."

"Mom and Dad are fighting."

"Come on. Don't let that worry you."

"I couldn't sleep."

I scoot over on my bed and she sits down, her nightgown pooling around her knees. She's washed all the makeup off and she got sunburned today, so she looks like my little sister again. It's something about winters and nighttimes that makes me remember how young Claudia is. It's when she's quiet. Her voice is old; she's always confused for our mother on the phone.

"Is this Camus stuff really any good?" she asks.

"He definitely knew his summers." I flip to one of my dog-eared pages. "'*Sometimes at night I would sleep open-eyed underneath a sky dripping with stars. I was alive then.'"*

She stares at me. "You can't sleep with your eyes open."

"You are so literal, Claude. Come on. Remember . . . you've got to remember. When Gid was still a baby, and Dad used to take me, you, and Noah and set us up on deck chairs on the balcony at night? Wrap us all up in sleeping bags and tell us stories? And we'd hear the waves come in and it would always be too bright to sleep—"

"Because of the stars?"

"Well, because Mom had all the lights on inside, walking Gideon up and down the hall so he'd shut up, but . . . yeah. The stars, too."

Claudia sticks her head out my window. "I mean, I don't know if they're *dripping* exactly."

"The sky's dripping."

She doesn't speak for a minute, then says, "Oh."

I tuck her under my arm and hold her for a while. She says, "I don't really remember."

"Well. You were young."

"Don't remember before Gideon." She smiles. "Was I alive then?"

"I assure you that you were."

"Your birthday's in two days."

"Oh, really? I didn't know."

She sticks out her tongue.

"Go back to bed," I say. "Gideon will feel you walking around and get all upset." Gid can tell the vibrations of our footsteps apart, and if he wakes up and realizes Claudia isn't in bed where she's supposed to be he is going to freak out. He hates when he wakes up and people aren't where they're supposed to be. Before he goes to bed every night, he takes an inventory of where we are, and if we drift, we have to be so quiet.

She kisses my cheek. "Night, Chase."

"Night."

"'*No love without a little innocence,*'" Noah says, completely still.

"I thought you were asleep. You're so creepy."

He shrugs. "So how was your lovely innocent night?"

"I kissed her."

"What a man." But he says it warmly. "How was it?"

My first thought is to relate it to soft-serve ice cream, but I can already hear Noah laughing at that. "It was nice."

"God. God, really, it was nice?" He sounds so earnest that I think for a minute that he's making fun of me. He props himself up on an elbow. "God, I fucking miss when kisses were nice. I'm so jealous of people young enough to still have nice kisses."

"Wait, kissing isn't nice anymore?"

"No. It's foreplay. Trust me, you get old enough, and everything is foreplay. Kissing is foreplay. Talking is foreplay. Holding hands is foreplay. I swear to God, Chase, I think at this point, sex would be foreplay."

This would probably be a good time to ask if he and Melinda have really slept together, but I can't make myself say the words. So I just say, "That doesn't even make sense."

"Sex is a to-do list where nothing gets crossed out."

I find the passage Melinda quoted in my Camus book. *"No love without a little innocence. Where was the innocence? Empires were tumbling down; nations and men were tearing at one another's throats; our hands were soiled. Originally innocent without knowing it, we were now guilty without meaning to be: the mystery was increasing our knowledge. This is why, O mockery, we were concerned with morality. Weak and disabled, I was dreaming of virtue!"*

Noah looks at me and coughs, his eyebrows up in his bangs.

"What?" I say.

With a straight face, he recites, *"'I may not have been sure about what really did interest me, but I was absolutely sure about what didn't.'"*

"Come on. It's *foreplay*? Seriously?"

"You're too young." He flops backward. "You wouldn't understand. You are a fetus in a world of Camus and spermicidal lubricant."

"And you're an asshole."

"I'm just cynical. And you have no idea how far that's going to take me."

"Neither do you."

"Au contraire, little brother. I know exactly how this college game works. I will arrive, the dark horse in a band of mushy-hearted freshman. College will pee itself in terror of my disenfranchised soul."

I roll my eyes. "Beautiful."

"Look. Listen to my words of wisdom. College's only role these days, for an upper-middle-class kid going in for a fucking liberal arts degree, is very simple. Do you know what that is?"

"A diploma. A good job. Yay."

"No. College exists only because it thrives on the hopes and dreams of the young and innocent. College is a hungry zombie here to eat your brains. It wants to remind you that your naivete is impermanent and someday, English major or no, you'll wear a suit and hate the feeling of sand between your toes."

It's not going to happen to me.

Noah continues, in a low mutter, "Like that's not already

forced into our heads every single fucking minute of every winter."

"So you're, like, essentially already educated, just because you're an asshole?"

"Because I've resigned myself to my fate, yeah. I've pre-colleged myself. I'm rocking the institution, entering it already all disillusioned and shit. I'm going to single-handedly change the world of higher education."

I clear my throat. *"'I may not have been sure about what really did interest me, but I was absolutely sure about what didn't.'"*

"Go to sleep. Asshole."

I never have a hard time falling asleep, but I do tonight. It takes a while of thinking of Bella's lips before I drift off.